SO-AMR-102

THE FABLES OF BORIS

THE FABLES OF BORIS

Invitations to Conversations between Children and Their Mentors

Richard Bellingham, EdD

iUniverse, Inc.
New York   Bloomington

The Fables of Boris
Invitations to Conversations between Children and Their Mentors

Copyright © 2009 by Richard Bellingham, EdD

All rights reserved. No part of this book may be used or reproduced by any means, graphic, electronic, or mechanical, including photocopying, recording, taping or by any information storage retrieval system without the written permission of the publisher except in the case of brief quotations embodied in critical articles and reviews.

This is a work of fiction. All of the characters, names, incidents, organizations, and dialogue in this novel are either the products of the author's imagination or are used fictitiously.

iUniverse books may be ordered through booksellers or by contacting:

iUniverse
1663 Liberty Drive
Bloomington, IN 47403
www.iuniverse.com
1-800-Authors (1-800-288-4677)

Because of the dynamic nature of the Internet, any Web addresses or links contained in this book may have changed since publication and may no longer be valid. The views expressed in this work are solely those of the author and do not necessarily reflect the views of the publisher, and the publisher hereby disclaims any responsibility for them.

ISBN: 978-1-4401-6245-9 (pbk)
ISBN: 978-1-4401-6247-3 (cloth)
ISBN: 978-1-4401-6246-6 (ebk)

iUniverse Rev Date: 10/14/2009
Printed in the United States of America

CONTENTS

▼

Acknowledgments

I gratefully acknowledge the contribution my daughters, Rebecca and Emily, made to this book. Without their love, support, inspiration, and superb editing capabilities, this book would have never been written.

I also wish to acknowledge the invaluable feedback provided by the parents and children who read the stories and shared their experiences with me. In particular, Bill O'Brien and his two children, Aidan and Liam, read every story and let me know what was working and not working. For instance, Aidan let me know in no uncertain terms that I had better get the spelling of his name correct. Peter Fasolo and his son, Alex, also read the stories diligently and shared their perspectives with me.

Finally, I want to thank Barry Cohen, a wise friend for forty years, for reading the stories and encouraging me to write guides to accompany each story.

Introduction

"Just one more Boris story."

This was the nightly plea I heard from my daughter just before bedtime. It meant another opportunity for me to conjure up a tale based on her experiences of the day. Trying to come from her frame of reference and using language she would understand, I used my imagination to create stories that might help her sort through whatever issue she might be facing.

Boris was a mythical character, a dog that happened to be experiencing the same life challenges as Rebecca did when she was a child, a time when every problem seemed like an overwhelming conundrum—or at least a terrific opportunity for some drama. Rebecca had always dreamed of becoming an actress, so every issue represented a chance for her to practice her drama skills. Serendipitously, while Boris initially had the same feelings and thoughts as Rebecca, he was always able to find the possible solutions that existed, no matter how hopeless the situation appeared through the eyes of a young girl.

Though I made up Boris stories for Rebecca throughout her childhood and adolescent years, the most intense time was when she was between the ages of eight and ten. This is a time in most kids' lives when they first begin to encounter significant social and emotional challenges, and yet it is a time when they are still open to talking about them with their parents.

Rebecca loved the Boris fables because they were entertaining and also enabled her to get a little distance from her concerns. She could get a new perspective on her world without feeling she was being lectured or that parental advice was being imposed upon her. I loved the Boris stories because they gave me an opportunity to crawl into my daughter's world and try to be helpful. Boris was the perfect medium through which to share "un-discussable topics" and to discover creative solutions to problems. Most importantly, the stories also served as a stimulus for engaging in meaningful conversation about important life issues.

When Rebecca turned ten, my wife and I adopted a second child from Korea. Emily was the most precious and adorable bundle of joy we could ever imagine. As she was growing up, I read a lot of books by Idries Shah, a prolific author of mystical literature, containing short stories describing the challenges Sufis faced as they tried to lead spiritual, holistic lives. Sufi stories drew upon the broad range of literature associated with the mystical arm of Islam identified primarily with Rumi, the twelfth-century poet. Contrary to many religions, Sufism is non-politicized, non-institutionalized, and is only interested in personal growth and development.

When Emily reached the age of eight, I started reading the Sufi stories to her. These stories always presented a spiritual knot that the reader was invited to untie. They did not spell out explanations of their endings but, like riddles, encouraged the audience—in this case Emily—to puzzle, question, and come up with her own explanations. She showed a remarkable ability to penetrate to the core of the message.

Unfortunately, my exclamations at her precocious ability led her to become self-conscious and withhold her interpretations. Emily experienced the praise as being put on the spot because she thought I was testing her. She continued, however, to enjoy the stories for several years, and they gave us an opportunity to discuss life issues in a very "unordinary" way.

Long after we had left the Sufi stories behind, Emily went on to Carnegie Mellon University, where she graduated in May of 2008. Her artist statement includes the Sufi stories as a formative part of her approach to art and to decision making in her life.

With our youngest child transitioning into independence, my wife and I are also moving into a new phase in our lives, giving us cause to both reflect on the past and look toward the future. After devoting thirty-seven years to teaching kids with learning disabilities, my wife retired in 2008. I am also slowing down my business as I approach retirement. We are both in our sixties now and, as prospective grandparents, our thoughts are on what we want to leave behind—not just for our own relatives, but for anyone who has children, cousins, students, or particularly smart dogs like Boris. When I would share these stories with my friends, they'd encourage me to write them down and publish them. That was twenty-four years ago, and I am only now taking up the challenge.

In many ways, my motivation for writing this book comes from my military intelligence experience in Vietnam from March of 1968 to March of 1969. I arrived in Saigon just after the Tet Offensive and was thrust immediately into the perils of war. While I was fortunate enough to have avoided the tunnels, jungles, and frontline fighting, I was confronted intimately with the devastating costs of war. In my visits to field hospitals, I would find young, inexperienced soldiers suffering from horrifying wounds and loss of limbs. I saw others suffer in other ways. I lost friends. The memories are still fresh in my mind.

My experience in Vietnam shocked me into thinking, "How could I best contribute to the creation of a more peaceful and harmonious world?" Over the past forty years, I have sought out every source of inspiration I could find that might lead to a solution. I have read and studied Nietzsche, Reich, Gurdjieff, Ouspensky, Carkhuff, and a whole range of philosophers from Latin America, Asia, Europe, and North America. I have studied the world religions and tried to find common elements among them. I have worked in jails, hospitals, drug abuse clinics, elementary schools, universities, and corporations trying to find ways to create healthy, innovative, and productive environments.

Finally, one year ago, it occurred to me that the best shot we have at making our kids understand the need to strive for harmony is to engage our youth in dialogue about the sanctity of life and the importance of growth and healing. I came to this realization from a combination of external and internal factors. Externally, I was overwhelmed by the violence occurring throughout the world. Internally, I was struck by the difficulty of trying to change behaviors after they were firmly entrenched as norms in the culture and as habits in the individual.

This is not an easy task in contemporary society. We are facing the ever-growing threat of extremist schools abroad and video games at home. As the tempo of life seems to speed up without limit, it becomes more and more difficult to take a pause from the rush forward and reflect upon our actions, thoughts, and feelings. Plus, the TV and the Internet do not serve us well as vehicles for active dialogue. Our children are at risk of becoming lost in cyberspace. As parents, teachers, and grandparents, we need to intervene.

But how? How do we get the attention of our youth when we are competing with so many more seductive and entertaining alternatives? Storytelling is a magical way of letting both teller and listener suspend disbelief and identify with characters, enriching understanding. The fables in this book are a way to speak on an equal level with a child, allowing meaningful discussions that add value to their lives. The stories present puzzles for kids to think about and to solve. Hopefully they will serve as a stimulus for engaging in meaningful conversations.

My biggest hope for this book is to transform the lessons I have learned over the course of my life into stories that are accessible to kids. I hope kids will be able to use Boris's tribulations to think through their own life issues in fresh, helpful, healing ways.

For example, one parent to whom I had given early versions of some of these stories to test with his kids came back to me with a note his eight-year-old son had written after reading one of the stories. It said, "Boris was trying to figure out a way to break free from his routines and find a way out of his prison. I need to do the same."

According to the child's father, this was the first time this child had ever written anything about a book and shared it with him. He was a quiet child, but he enjoyed having the opportunity to read together with his father and talk about the issues.

The main goal of these stories is to help adults connect with children in meaningful ways. Sharing your own experience and demonstrating understanding of the child's experience are the two best ways to forge that connection. The parent guides at the start of each chapter will help you prepare for each conversation by reflecting upon your own experience and by looking for the main ideas in each story. While every child will react differently to each story, the guides will help you and the child understand your own and each other's point of view and philosophy of life regarding the fable.

An overview of the learning objectives and life skills for each story is contained in the appendix of this book. The following five-step process will help the adult be as helpful to the child as possible:

Clarify your understanding of how the child experiences the story. Practice active listening by rephrasing the child's thoughts in your own words. Use simple, easy-to-understand language.

Filter through the child's reactions to determine the most meaningful issue to them. Let the child guide the discussion, but listen for cues that seem most relevant and significant to the child—the cues that could lead to a "high-impact" moment.

Respond to the feelings that issue evokes and the meaning it holds for the child.

Share your point of view and experience in dealing with the issue. Use the questions in the parent reflection section of each guide to help you articulate your experience clearly and to connect your perspective to the child's experience.

Engage in creative thinking with the child to find the optimal solution for their own situation. Brainstorm ways of dealing with issues or achieving goals.

The overall purpose of telling, sharing, and discussing these stories is to enrich the spiritual lives of children. Hopefully, through the conversation process, you will be able to strengthen your connection and deepen your insight into the passions and dreams of the children you love.

A Note of Caution

At the end of each mentor guide, there is a list of questions that you may find yourself engaged in after reading the story. However, it is important that these stories don't turn into interrogation sessions with the child. If the child feels put on the spot by a question, then he or she will probably close down. In order to free the child to explore and to deepen their understanding of their own experience, you need to follow the child's lead, not lead them to where you want to go.

The minute the conversation turns into you forwarding your agenda—even if you're only trying to help—will be the minute you have lost the possibility for connection and spiritual development. Ideally, the child will ask *you* these questions, instead of you posing the questions to the child. You want the child to direct the conversation and to choose discussion topics.

In the first story, it is as important to hook the child on the content as it is to hook him or her on the process. You want the child to get excited about the adventures of Boris, and you want him or her to value the idea of reading a story together and talking about it. Some parents read the story to the child, and others have the child read the story first and then talk about it. Seek understanding together. It will be an exciting adventure.

You and the child will realize early on in the book that Boris has both human and canine characteristics. Boris sometimes acts like a dog by digging in the dirt, rolling on the ground, wagging his tail, and so on. But at other times, Boris takes on human characteristics like thinking, talking, relating a story, or planning. The intent is to make Boris completely fictional and fanciful and to give the child some distance from the problems we face as human beings. Telling the story from the dog's frame of reference is an attempt to engage the child in processing important life lessons without feeling threatened or scared by the challenges he or she will face growing up.

Lastly, remember that enjoying the book is a vital part of the process. While these fables are meant to help children navigate through certain life issues, they are also meant to be fun and engaging. Make the experience a positive one for you and your loved ones, and the lessons will teach themselves.

Guide for Chapter 1:

▼

Boris's New Life Starts with a Thud

In this opening story, Boris begins his quest for spiritual development and growth. He has to deal with an abrupt and scary beginning to his journey.

In preparation for this first conversation, reflect on your own life experience. Think about key points in your life when an event, expected or unexpected, caused you to change the way you look at the world. When have you experienced an emotional thud? The event could be positive or negative. The thud may have been when a parent or good friend died and you realized that not only would life no longer be the same for you, but also that life does not last forever. Also review the biggest choices you have had to make in your life.

This story opens the book with a violent and socially irresponsible act that no amount of sugarcoating or sentimentalizing can excuse. In many ways this book is an attempt to reduce violence and increase social responsibility by sensitizing kids to these acts and preparing them at an early age to recognize what kindness and compassion look like.

The story raises questions about several issues:

➢ Making decisions

➢ Staying calm in a crisis

➢ Looking for possibilities in even the worst situations

➢ Taking the initiative to make things happen in your life

In my experience working with children, I have found that each child reacts differently to a given story. Some may want to talk about the unfairness of being abandoned. Others may want to talk about how hard it was for Boris to stay focused after the event. Still others may inquire about how Boris made his choice to walk toward the lake instead of getting back on the highway. Please remember, I make no claims on having found "the best answer." All we can do is seek the best answer for each of us and our individual situations. I believe that is best accomplished through dialogue.

As a result of responding to this story, you might find yourself engaged with the child in any or all of these questions:

- What is Boris's quest?

- Why did Boris decide to go down the hill instead of cross the road?

- What is Boris's attitude toward life?

- How do you think Boris felt when he heard another dog at the end of the street?

CHAPTER 1

▼

BORIS'S NEW LIFE STARTS WITH A THUD

"Boris, you're a sweet puppy, and we love you, but there are just too many mouths to feed in this family. We're going to have to drop you off in a nice neighborhood and hope you are able to find a kind family who will take you in."

The puppy's owner, a young woman with three kids and several other pets, had just lost her job. She opened the car door and dropped Boris gently to the ground. She had placed a name tag around Boris's neck with a note attached saying, "Boris is looking for a good home. I hope you will give him one."

In a choked-up voice and with teary eyes, she said, "Good luck, little puppy. We know you are a special dog and you will find your way. We will miss you."

Thud—Boris was on his own.

Boris, only two months old and looking like a brown, curly fur ball, felt his legs tremble. His eyes grew wide as he checked out his new surroundings: open fields, huge trees, a large hill, a beautiful lake, and tall weeds. He started walking carefully along the road looking for a friendly face. Boris was faced with his first choice in this new, suddenly scary and uncertain life. He could cross the major highway and head up a small hill to where he saw a big, brick building, or he could start walking down a steep road that led to a gorgeous, blue lake in the distance.

As he stared across the highway toward the building uphill, a huge truck whizzed past. All Boris could see from his little body on the ground were giant wheels spinning dangerously and throwing stones. It didn't take him long to make his choice. Like a magnet, Boris felt the pull of the cool, blue waters.

As Boris stumbled down the hill, calming his heart and steadying his paws, he passed by a large, red farmhouse with fenced-in fields and several small houses set away from the road. Halfway to the lake, Boris felt a flea on his back. Soon he was spinning around in circles trying to gnaw the irritating pest away.

"Ahh, I got it!" Boris sighed with relief once he'd scared the bug away. "But now I need to get back to my task." Not seeing any inviting signs, like playing children, abandoned toys, or food on a porch, Boris continued his search. His quest for something more in life had begun.

Being alone in a strange place made Boris nervous, but calming his fears, he felt more and more sure-footed as he trotted down the hill. As the lake came into clearer focus, so did his thoughts and feelings. Pausing at the bottom of the hill and surveying his surroundings, Boris gave himself permission to hope for an exciting new life in this unknown place. He admired the scenery before him: windblown fields to his right that stretched for what seemed like miles before they ran up to a dense, mysterious pine forest. He loved the contrast between the deep, blue water and the rich, green leaves on the trees.

But now, near the lakefront right in front of him, he had to make another choice. He could take a left turn down a paved street or a right turn down a dirt path lined with trees. He hadn't wondered long when he heard what sounded like a friendly dog's bark in the distance off to the right. He made his choice.

As Boris walked hesitantly down the dirt road, he passed a few more houses. His confidence grew as he spotted doghouses in some of the yards. Boris started panting hard with excitement, his tongue darting quickly in and out of his mouth. He took a deep breath and continued his journey. The barking grew louder.

"Lucky, stop that barking!" Mr. Knowles yelled out the door, not knowing that Lucky had seen another dog crossing in front of the house. Lucky charged toward the road with fur flying every which way and then came to a screeching halt, his tail wagging rapidly. Fortunately, he had stopped barking in response to Mr. Knowles's command, which eased Boris's fears.

"Whew," Boris panted a sigh of relief. "Maybe someday he'll be my friend," he thought as he slinked past the house.

When Lucky noticed that Boris was just a harmless puppy, he barked more gently to him. "Hey, you can come stay with me if you're lost," the friendly dog said.

"Daddy, Mommy!" shouted two young boys before Boris could respond. The kids, aged three and five, lived in the brown, two-story house next door to Lucky's house. It was at the very end of the street. "It's the sweetest little dog. Please, can we keep him? Look how nervous and hungry he looks. Oh please, Daddy?"

Boris wiggled his way shyly up to the boys and licked their hands. Mr. Hamm, as the man was called, looked at his wife, shrugged his shoulders, nodded his head, and said, "Okay, boys."

And just like that, Boris had found his new home. His quest was off to a good start.

GUIDE FOR CHAPTER 2:

▼

BORIS SETTLES IN TO HIS NEW NEIGHBORHOOD

In this story, the child is introduced to the context in which Boris will pursue his quest for a full life. This chapter describes the house in which Boris will be living, the family he will be living with, and the neighborhood dogs who will play major roles throughout the book.

In preparation for your conversation about this story, think about the biggest adventure you've ever had. Was it, perhaps, moving into a new neighborhood, going on a vacation, or exploring an exciting new career?

The first possible discussion topic this chapter poses is the whole idea of how new people are welcomed into a community. In this story, the family and the neighborhood dogs all go out of their way to be supportive, kind, and helpful. Your children might want to talk about an experience during which they did not feel welcome and how they dealt with that.

Second, the challenge of dealing with new places, new people, and new rules could come up in your conversation. It's important to stress how useful it is to size up a situation before making too many bold moves. Also, in all situations, it's critical to know what the "rules" are. That doesn't mean that one has to follow all the social rules, but you should know what they are and what the consequences are for breaking them.

It's also possible that a child might want to talk about the differences among all the dogs. Gabby is fun and friendly. Prudence tends to be more prim and proper. Lucky is always kind and supportive. Another difference that the child might notice is that not all dogs appear to be kind. The underlying tension from an unnamed gang of dogs raises new alarms and questions about what you do when there is a bully on the block.

As a result of responding to this story, you might find yourself engaged with the child in any or all of these questions:

- What was the biggest adventure you have ever thought about?

- When have you unknowingly broken expected rules and been scolded for it?

- Who do you think will be Boris's best friend? Why?

- Where, in life, do you feel welcome?

- Where don't you feel welcome all the time?

CHAPTER 2

▼

BORIS SETTLES IN TO HIS NEW NEIGHBORHOOD

Boris was thrilled with his new home. The Hamms, who adopted him, were immediately delighted with his playful antics. Mr. Hamm, a teacher at the local school, loved to play sports with his sons, Liam and Aidan, and he laughed out loud at the way Boris begged each of them to throw the ball to him. Mrs. Hamm, a doctor in a local clinic, enjoyed watching Liam and Aidan chase Boris all around the yard as the puppy cleverly evaded them. Inside, Boris would proudly prance around the house with a stick he had found.

Whenever Boris got excited, his eyes opened wide, and he wiggled all over. The Hamm boys thought Boris was the most adorable puppy they had ever seen. Liam screamed with delight when Boris licked his face every time he picked him up. Aidan jumped with joy when Boris ran into the kitchen and skidded across the hardwood floors. Boris thought, "How could I be so lucky to find a home where the people love me and there is plenty of room to play?"

The Hamm fam, as Boris called them, lived at the end of a dirt road in the middle of the woods. The house had a sunny, screened-in porch, a serene deck overlooking the woods, and an open living area with a cozy fireplace. But from Boris's point of view, the best thing about his new home was not the inside—it was all the wilderness around it that invited adventure. The big lake at one end of the street seemed to call, "Boris, come in for a swim!" The small beaver pond at the end of a mile-long trail through the woods at the other end of the street was alive with activity that made Boris's ears perk up with the possibilities. To top it off, several other houses on the street also had dogs, so Boris couldn't wait to start making friends.

After Boris got adjusted to his new home and learned the new rules—no chewing on the furniture, no peeing on the rug, no jumping on guests—he yearned to go outside and get acquainted with all the neighborhood animals. Boris pranced across the yard and boldly walked right up to the neighbor's door. In his eagerness to meet new friends, he crashed right through the neighbor's pristine garden, knocking a few tomatoes off the vines.

Being just a puppy, Boris was surprised when the neighbor abruptly flung open the door with a serious scowl on his face. Mr. Knowles was proud of his garden and got angry when anyone disturbed the neat rows or ruined any of his precious plants. Boris's turbo tail suddenly went limp, and he cowered a bit on the porch, his knees as shaky as his sense of security. Mr. Knowles, quickly realizing that Boris didn't know any better, turned his scowl into a smile and called for Lucky.

Suddenly, the bigger dog that Boris had met briefly the other day came bounding out onto the porch. Boris brightened up. Lucky jumped around Boris, hoping this new dog would prove to be a fun-loving friend. Boris remembered that Lucky had been kind to him when he first stumbled into the neighborhood. The slightly older puppy had a soft, shiny, black coat and expressive, kind eyes. Boris was amazed at the size of Lucky's paws—they were huge compared to his own puppy paws.

After Lucky and Boris chased each other around the yard for a while, Lucky was satisfied that Boris would be a welcome addition to the neighborhood. He offered to introduce Boris to the other dogs in the neighborhood.

A few doors down, Lucky and Boris found Prudence playing out in her family's yard. Prudence was a small, white dog with curly fur and a pointy nose. Boris also noticed she was wearing a red ribbon in her fur. He was a bit curious what that was all about, but he decided not to ask about it. Not yet, anyway. Prudence seemed dainty and often held her nose high in the air. While Boris thought she might be boringly prim and proper, he was impressed by her obvious refinement. Boris sensed that Prudence might have some deep talent behind her surface features.

Prudence looked deeply into Boris's eyes with a thoughtful frown on her face. Lucky interrupted Boris's train of thought by introducing them. "Prudence, this is Boris. He's a new dog on the block, just moved in with the Hamm family."

Ever-polite Prudence welcomed Boris to the neighborhood and said she would be pleased to have tea and dog biscuits with him one day.

Lucky, a bit impatient, said, "Well, we'll have to get going. Lots more friends to meet. See ya, Pru!"

Boris and Lucky made a quick exit and strolled down the road. Before long, they arrived at Gabby's house. Gabby was a young, friendly dog with beautiful brown fur. She was taking a nap in her backyard, but she jumped up eagerly when she heard Boris and Lucky approach. She barked a warm welcome and immediately started sniffing Boris to make his acquaintance. Gabby bounced around the yard with her tail wagging and her ears flopping. Boris thought, "I like her energy and enthusiasm! I hope we'll be good friends." After a quick game of tag and chase, Lucky, Gabby, and Boris plopped down on the grass for a little rest and some chatting.

Boris was beaming with happiness over his new friends. Once again, he couldn't believe his good luck. "Is every dog in this neighborhood as nice as you guys?" he asked with wide eyes.

A serious look settled onto Lucky's face as he explained that that was not the case. He cautioned Boris against getting involved with some of the neighborhood gangs that had been forming over the past year. These gangs consisted of dogs that had not been well cared for and had had to survive on their own. They often attacked other dogs for no apparent reason.

Gabby nodded in agreement and then warned Boris of another danger. She told him he should not to do his business on Mrs. Sharpie's lawn or dig in her yard. Mrs. Sharpie took great pride in her bright green, weed-free lawn and could be very nasty to trespassing dogs.

But Boris couldn't stop thinking about Lucky's warning, wondering who these ominous other dogs could be and how to tell them apart from potential friends. He remembered Prudence's reserved tone and unmoving tail and how unsure he felt around her. "Is Prudence in one of those gangs?" he asked.

Both Gabby and Lucky assured Boris that, although Prudence could be a little standoffish at first, she was really okay in their book. She definitely was on the approved buddy list.

Suddenly, Boris yawned and felt tiredness seep into his bones. He decided to trot back to his new home and relax by himself. Slowly pulling himself up, Boris thanked Lucky and Gabby and said he was going home for a nap. As he made his way home on the dirt road, he thought, "This was a very good day. I like this neighborhood, even if I do need to watch out for groups of mean dogs."

GUIDE FOR CHAPTER 3:

▼

BORIS FINDS A WISE FRIEND

In this story, Boris stumbles into Zelda, another key figure in the book. Zelda is a wise dog with an old soul. She has profound insights and deep perspective on the big issues in life. Boris learns there are dogs from whom he has a lot to learn.

In preparation for your conversation after reading this chapter, think about who your mentors in life have been. Who do you go to when you have a life issue on which you want a thoughtful perspective? Also, do you identify with your role? That is, are you strongly identified as a mother, father, or teacher? How does this identification affect your openness to new ideas?

This story addresses two critical issues in life:

➢ Overidentifying can cause close-mindedness

➢ Trusted friends are an important asset in life.

This story also raises questions about overcoming fears that could keep you from experiencing life fully. It further demonstrates the effect a person can have on you by being calm and respectful and by really listening to what you have to say.

Finally, this story illustrates how time can pass very rapidly in some instances and extremely slowly in other instances. It's important for the child to get a sense of what makes time pass quickly or slowly. Why does time goes so fast when you are fully engaged and so slow when you are full of fear?

As a result of responding to this story, you might find yourself engaged with the child in any or all of these questions:

- Have you ever felt shaky when you started a new adventure?

- Have you ever had to find courage in the face of fear?

- Why did Boris get the feeling that Zelda would be a great friend?

- Why did the trip home seem so different from the trip out?

CHAPTER 3

▼

BORIS FINDS A WISE FRIEND

After two weeks in his new home, Boris decided it was time to venture into the mysterious woods on his own. Liam and Aidan had taken him on walks to show him around the neighborhood, and they had led him down the trail in the woods so that he could get a quick look at the beaver pond. Although anxious to explore the wild unknown, he had been waiting to find the courage to blindly set forth.

Boris was not sure where his journey might lead or what he might find along the way. Trembling as he inched his way down the path, he began to feel overwhelmed by the large trees that surrounded him, particularly as he made his way farther and farther from the safety of his home. Birch, maple, pine, and poplar trees all grew randomly in a wild tangle of leaves and limbs that eerily swayed, making strange, creaking noises. There were white trees with pointy, green leaves; brown trees with prickly, red leaves; and gray trees with crinkly, orange leaves.

Boris started gaining confidence as he continued shakily, but steadily, down the trail. Even though his body felt tense and tingly in anticipation of what surprises or horrors he might find, he was calmed by the comforting canopy the trees provided and by the shafts of light that streamed through it, breaking up the darkness of the woods. As he went deeper into the woods, there were hills to climb, swamps to avoid, and ridges that blocked his view.

Suddenly, a squirrel darted in front of him, scrambled up a tree, and started to chatter right at Boris from a branch that was high out of his reach. This was Boris's first ever squirrel sighting, and he stared, fascinated by the creature's quick, sharp movements and scolding voice. Then a flock of birds swooped through the woods, startling Boris. As they passed low overhead, he'd felt like they were dive-bombing him. His confidence began to slip. He noticed that his tail was hanging between his legs and his ears were flat against his head. He was stopped, uncharacteristically motionless, but then he summoned up his courage and proceeded down the trail once more.

Soon, to his surprise, a bright space emerged out of the darkness of the forest path. He found an open clearing with a sparkling, fresh, clear stream with a makeshift bridge spanning it. Boris crossed over the stream and pushed ahead. He found that the trail had twists and turns at every juncture. He jumped over (or slid under) logs, avoided underbrush, and navigated the sharp turns. Trusting his instincts as a dog, Boris wasn't too worried about getting lost, but he was still in suspense about what might lie ahead.

After what seemed like hours (but was actually only fifteen minutes), Boris came to the remote beaver pond tucked into the forest. He was fascinated by the bustling activities of the beavers, who had cut down whole trees with their teeth and built a home for themselves in the pond. The beaver house looked like a mountain of sticks piled high along the bank of the pond. It shut out the light from above and created an internal world for the beavers to live in. Boris wondered what it must be like to live under the sticks at the edge of the pond.

The shallow pond had scattered trees that served as nesting points and perching spots for all kinds of colorful birds. Boris spotted ducks, swallows, and even an eagle sitting regally atop one of the trees.

A strange voice made Boris jump. His eyes widened as he tried in vain to locate the source. A dog—who looked kind, to his relief—had appeared from the shadows and was trying to introduce herself. She was a medium-sized, brown dog with curly hair and sparkling eyes. "I'm Zelda," she said, repeating her greeting now that she had Boris's attention. "I live on the other side of the pond. I've never seen you in this neck of the woods. You must be new. Welcome."

Boris relaxed. Zelda's voice had a calming influence on him. Boris knew immediately that Zelda was special. She moved slowly and showed great interest in him. He looked forward to getting to know her. He noticed that his tail had started wagging and that his ears were no longer glued to his head.

Though they had only just met, Boris learned a lot about Zelda that day. She was an intriguing dog because, unlike the other dogs he had met, Zelda didn't identify with any particular breed. She was a little bit of a lot of breeds. And she didn't mind being different or particularly unidentifiable as a type. To Zelda, breed didn't matter.

Even in a short amount of time, Boris found that he admired Zelda because she loved to think. Talking to Zelda gave Boris a sense of freedom he hadn't experienced before. She had the unique ability to stay calm, be attentive, and be respectful of Boris's obvious youth and inexperience.

In some ways, Boris found his conversation with Zelda confusing because she sat so still and gave very few reactions (like wiggling around, barking, and perking up her ears—all the things Boris did constantly). Yet she seemed to listen intently to everything Boris said. On another level, Boris felt peaceful being with Zelda exactly *because* she seemed so content to sit quietly and didn't find it necessary to run frantically from one activity to another, like Boris often did.

Zelda asked great questions: "What's your favorite thing to do at the Hamm house? How are you getting along with Lucky? Have you spotted any of the gangs hanging around the neighborhood?" She asked questions about Boris that he hadn't thought about before. "What's it like living with two young kids who always want to play? What makes you trust the Hamms so completely?"

And Boris enjoyed answering her questions. It helped him sort out for himself how he was feeling and why he was feeling that way.

After talking to Zelda for what seemed like minutes (it was actually two hours), Boris felt his stomach growl and noticed that his mouth was dry. He had come a long way through the woods, which no longer seemed so terrifying, and he had met a very wise friend. He knew that now he needed to find his way home and fill his stomach. "Zelda, it's time for me to go home," he explained when their conversation hit a stopping point.

"Well, it was nice to meet you," replied Zelda.

With that, Boris pranced gaily back to the Hamm fam. He had no trouble following the trail home and was surprised how differently the trip back felt from the trip out. It seemed shorter, clearer, and less foreboding. Relaxed, his gait sure-footed and carefree, Boris wondered for a moment why the trip home felt so different. However, he quickly pushed aside the question at the first sight of home.

GUIDE FOR CHAPTER 4:

▼

BORIS BREAKS THE RULES

Now that most of the main characters have been introduced and the context described, we can dive into some of the life issues we all confront. The remaining stories all describe challenges that children—indeed, everyone— has to deal with as they grow up and develop. Older children hopefully will be able to dive deeper into these complex issues. The extent to which we have thought about these challenges as children prepares us to make the right choices later in life.

In preparation for the conversation you and the child have about this story, you may want to think about times in your life where you found "the rules" overly restrictive and confining in how they affected your state of being. How were you able to deal with those restrictions?

In this story, Mr. and Mrs. Hamm are dealing with one of the most crucial decisions for parents: when do we free our children, and when do we try to control them? The Hamms are trying to decide how much freedom to give Boris. The kids argue for more freedom and fewer rules, while the parents struggle with how much control they should enforce. Clearly, the kids hold a different point of view on who is to blame for Boris's bad behavior. In the end, the parents decide to forgive Boris for his puppylike misdeeds, and all turns out well.

In my experience raising two wonderful children, I have usually erred on the side of giving too much freedom and not exerting enough control. As I look back on those decisions, I don't regret them at all. I still have loving relationships with both children, and they have grown into thoughtful, responsible adults.

As a result of responding to this story, you might find yourself engaged with the child in any or all of these questions:

- When have you broken a rule? What happened as a result?

- Have you ever been in a situation in which you felt you were unfairly blamed?

- What happens when you accuse someone of doing something they didn't do?

- Have you ever forgiven someone for doing something that hurt you? How did you feel as a result?

CHAPTER 4

▼

BORIS BREAKS THE RULES

At first, the Hamms were so pleased to have Boris's playful energy in the house that they overlooked his occasional breaking of a rule. They were sure he would calm down once he settled in and began to grow older. He had been chewing on the furniture, tipping over flower vases as he sprinted from room to room in his wild enthusiasm, and had recently left a "gift" on the living room rug. According to Boris, this last problem was the Hamm's fault because they hadn't let him out of the house in time.

But Boris's energy only seemed to increase, while his care for the house rules seemed to shrink. By the end of the first couple months, the Hamms became increasingly annoyed with Boris. Mrs. Hamm, a tall, pretty woman with kind, brown eyes who was normally low-key and easy to get along with, finally decided to institute a whole new set of rules.

"From now on," Mrs. Hamm announced at dinner that night, "Boris will not be allowed in the living room, he will not be allowed on any furniture, he will have to sleep in his cage at night, and he will have to go outside immediately in the morning for fifteen minutes. There will be *no* exceptions to these rules," she said sternly as she looked around the table, fixing her gaze on the two Hamm boys.

Liam and Aidan were visibly upset; their faces were scrunched, their fists were clenched, and they had deep frowns on their faces. "Those rules are so unfair!" whined Liam. "He's just a puppy."

"If we play with him in the living room, he won't chew on the leg of your antique table," Aidan pleaded.

But Mrs. Hamm wasn't budging an inch. "We need to have rules until Boris learns who *does* rule in this house," she said emphatically. "The truth is that Boris gets excited and can't contain himself, but he has to learn, puppy or not. He's been with us for two months now, and he hasn't gotten any better."

Liam continued to plead his case. "But, Mom, you were the one who said puppies need to play. And besides, you didn't let him out in the morning today."

Mr. Hamm intervened. "Boys, I know you are sad because you love your dog, and you want him to be happy. What you need to understand is that we can't afford to replace all of the furniture in our house because Boris likes to chew on it."

Liam and Aidan knew that their parents were right, but also that they loved Boris and had no intentions of punishing him unfairly. "You can't rely on rules for everything," Aidan said defiantly. "Maybe we just need to have a talk with Boris."

Boris was lying flat on the ground at the foot of the table with his ears flat on his head. His eyes moved between Mr. and Mrs. Hamm and Liam and Aidan as they had their conversation about him. Boris knew that he was in big trouble because Mr. and Mrs. Hamm kept looking at him with scowling glares, while Liam and Aidan would look at Boris with pouting faces and sad eyes. Distressed, Boris closed his own eyes and awaited the worst.

Just then, Mrs. Hamm approached Boris and kneeled down beside him. As she patted his head, his tail started swiping slowly back and forth on the floor. "Boris," she said, "I can tell you feel bad because your eyes are so droopy and your chin is flat on the floor. I haven't seen you sit this still since you first came to our house."

Boris's ears came to attention as he slowly dragged himself off the floor and stood up on shaky legs. He was sure the Hamms would never love him again. Boris was even anxious that they might give him away.

"We still love you, Boris," Mrs. Hamm continued, "but we need to add a few rules until you grow up a little more. You are still too young to have complete run of this house. When you learn to go to the bathroom outside and to chew on your bone instead of my favorite tables and shoes, then we can loosen up the rules." Boris licked her hand and wagged his tail appreciatively.

Mrs. Hamm didn't realize that Boris had actually understood everything she had said. Unbeknownst to her, Boris was thinking to himself, "Whew, I got lucky today! Not only am I staying, but I don't have to go to my cage for time-out!" Boris quickly jumped up and gave Mrs. Hamm a big lick on the face.

"Oh, Boris," Mrs. Hamm chuckled, "you just can't help being a bad dog, can you?" Boris saw the twinkle in her eye and knew he was safe. He bounded over to Liam and Aidan. He knew who his two best allies in the whole world were.

GUIDE FOR CHAPTER 5:

▼

BORIS ASSESSES HIS CURRENT LIFE

This story is about pain and possibility. As parents, we sometimes numb ourselves to the pain we are feeling so we don't have to act—whether it's the death of someone close to us or the demise of a relationship, or sometimes we are simply afraid to open up to new possibilities in our lives because we would then feel pressured to pursue them. The challenge is to assess accurately both pain and possibilities for ourselves and our children—the pain of continuing in the present state and the possibility of creating a new state. This is not an easy task. You need to be open to the whole truth.

In preparation for your conversation after reading this chapter, reflect upon times in your life when you were so caught up in the flow of daily routines and responsibilities that you failed to notice all the possibilities and wonders that were constantly unfolding in your life. What did it take for you to openly embrace your possibilities, to take a hard look at your pain, and to make a disciplined effort to grow?

In this story, Boris observes how all his friends stew in their present realities and/or ignore their possibilities. The story raises the question about how you seek possibilities responsibly—that is, meeting your obligations, resisting reckless risks, and staying focused on the possibility all at the same time. Thanks to Zelda, Boris also learns to appreciate the fact that it is much easier to see the speck in someone else's eye than it is to see the log in your own. Finally, Boris learns that it's a good idea to seek counsel on difficult issues.

As a result of responding to this story, you might find yourself engaged with the child in any or all of these questions:

- When you are so busy trying to deal with all the responsibilities in your life (such as homework, chores, sports, arts, etc.), how do you find time to reflect upon what might be possible in your life?

- Of all your friends, which ones do you think are really being proactive in their lives?

- Does it ever bug you when your friends seem to be perfectly content with the way things are and refuse to do anything to make things better?

- What are your dreams for your life?

- Why is it sometimes so hard to find the time or make the effort to do what you really want to do?

- What do you believe are your greatest strengths?

CHAPTER 5

▼

BORIS ASSESSES HIS CURRENT LIFE

Boris was restless. It had only been three months since he moved into his new neighborhood, and he already thought his friends, nice as they were, led boring lives. He pictured Lucky lounging on his porch all day soaking up the sun. Lucky would wag his tail wildly whenever he got a treat and then slouch back down, breathe a big sigh, and collapse on the porch again. Gabby spent her whole day socializing with her friends. She would talk with Prudence for hours and then stroll to the next house and have the same conversation with another dog.

Boris wasn't sure if either of them thought much about how their lives were going, as long as they had enough to eat every day. Ever since Boris was dropped off and left to fend for himself, he knew it was up to him to make the most of his life. He intended to take advantage of the good fortune of accidentally stumbling upon the Hamm fam—he could have ended up in a much worse situation, with mean parents, whining kids, and no friendly dogs in the neighborhood.

Boris loved to imagine freely and wildly and create new possibilities in his mind. Sometimes he would get so caught up in fantastic possibilities that he would ignore the essential realities in his life. Like sometimes, Boris would get lost in thought about his next adventure in the woods, his next swim in the lake, or his next visit with Zelda, and he would forget to pick up the paper at the end of the driveway—one of his primary responsibilities.

Boris knew that if the Hamm fam didn't have their morning paper, they could be grumpy. He might even forget to bark when a stranger came near to the house, which could put the family he loved in possible danger. Boris was also responsible for licking up the crumbs on the floor that Liam and Aidan dropped during dinner. He looked forward to this task every meal. In fact, he took this job so seriously that he would lie under the table and wait for a choice scrap to fall from the table—either accidentally or intentionally.

Still, Boris was constantly searching for new possibilities and telling everyone what he had been thinking about. On windy days, Boris imagined what it would be like to borrow a sailboat and sail across the lake. On playful days, he would create a new game to play in the woods. But to his surprise and disappointment, not everyone was really interested in his crazy ideas.

To Boris, Lucky seemed stuck in the same boring routine he went through every day. Lucky would wake up in the morning, stretch his legs, shake his head, wag his tail, bark three times, and go to the Knowles's bedroom door, where he would lie down and wait for them to wake up. If they took too long, Lucky would scratch on their door.

Sometimes, Lucky got in big trouble for disturbing his family. Mr. Knowles would stumble out of bed, grab Lucky by his collar, and drag him to the garage. "I don't want to hear another sound from you!" Mr. Knowles might bark—not like a dog would bark, but like humans sometimes do when they are irritated.

When the Knowles family finally got out of bed, Lucky would eagerly lick their hands and wiggle all over to let them know he was excited to see them. He would then go outdoors and use his private bathroom. When Mr. Knowles called him back inside, he'd run obediently right to the door because he knew breakfast would soon be served. The rest of his day always followed the same pattern: go for a walk, take a nap, bark at the cat, dig a hole, sit on the porch, have dinner, watch TV, and go back to his bed. To Boris, Lucky's life seemed much too routine, particularly compared to his own life.

Every day, Boris would dream up an exciting new way to enjoy his day. Just yesterday, Boris challenged himself to find twenty different kinds of birds in the woods.

Like Lucky, Gabby also had rigid daily routines. But unlike Lucky, she felt dissatisfied and trapped by them. Every time Boris sauntered over to Gabby's yard to play, he sympathized with her. "Then again," he thought, "her problem is because she's confined to her cage during the night. And during the day, she's put on a chain while the Krafts are at work."

Gabby enjoyed the time she did get to spend with Mr. and Mrs. Kraft jogging before work or hanging out with them as they read the paper before bed. But Boris felt terrible that Gabby had so little freedom in her life. In fact, he would regularly trot over to Gabby's house and keep her company during the day when she was on a chain.

"Every day feels the same. I have nowhere to go," she would sigh. "Fortunately, Prudence comes to visit, my chain is long enough for me to roam a bit, and you are always there for me. Still, I just don't feel satisfied."

Boris noticed, though, that she had trouble inventing possible solutions to her problems. In contrast, Boris found it easy and fun to constantly scheme up ways to make his life better—like this morning when he and his feline friend, Sally Siamese, chased rabbits. Even though Gabby was stuck on her chain, she seemed unable to even think of ways to liven up her life, despite being unhappy.

Boris was confused by both Lucky and Gabby because they looked at the world in such different ways even though they were both house dogs. Lucky didn't seem to give any thought to how things were going in his life, and Gabby seemed unable to make her wish for a more enjoyable life become a reality. She would have preferred to have lots of dogs at her house every day because there was no such thing as too much social time for her.

Boris decided to ask his new friend, Zelda, what she thought about this. "How can Lucky and Gabby be so stuck in their lives?" he asked.

Zelda had been taking an afternoon nap under a big, shady tree. She slowly stretched, looked at Boris, smiled, and said, "Some dogs get so caught in the realities of their day-to-day lives that they can't see any possibilities for improvement. Other dogs are so inspired by their possibilities that they lose touch with their realities and responsibilities ... like you, Boris. And then there are a few clever dogs who are fully in touch with their realities but who continue to look for possibilities. Everyone is capable of doing this, but not everyone does; it takes constant work, attention, and awareness."

Boris scratched his ear with his left paw and looked at Zelda with admiration. He had never seen himself as, in a way, being guilty of the same flaw that he saw in Lucky and Gabby—his approach was just another side of the same coin. Boris heaved a huge sigh. "It sounds so simple when you say it, Zelda, but it's such a hard thing for me to do. I know I need to achieve a better balance between staying grounded and not getting stuck in a rut. All I know is that having you as a friend makes my life go better."

GUIDE FOR CHAPTER 6:

▼

BORIS MAKES A PLAN

This story is about pursuing your dreams. In it, Boris lets his imagination run wild and then confronts reality.

In preparation for this conversation, reflect upon the dreams you had as a child. Did the dreams represent a higher purpose, or were they more self-indulgent? Did you have goals? How did you go about setting those goals? How did you deal with the inevitable setbacks that we all experience in the pursuit of our dreams, ambitions, and passions?

As you can see from the questions above, there's a lot going on this story. There are several issues on which you and the child could focus depending upon how he or she reacts to the story:

➢ Setting goals

➢ Finding the right teacher

➢ Assessing your talents

➢ Dealing with setbacks

➢ Giving honest feedback

As a parent, I have always tried to support my children's dreams, even when I knew their decisions would probably lead to heartbreak and tough times. While both children encountered difficult challenges, they managed to work through them and to move on with few regrets.

As a result of responding to this story, you might find yourself engaged with the child in any or all of these questions:

- What are your dreams?

- Have you ever become impatient when things didn't go the way you hoped they would?

- Who has been the most important teacher in your life?

- How have you dealt with setbacks in the past?

- Who do you go to for honest feedback?

CHAPTER 6

▼

BORIS MAKES A PLAN

Boris had just celebrated his first anniversary with the Hamm fam, and he figured he needed some higher goals in his life. "I have the most fun when I'm jumping and playing," he pondered. And in a flash, Boris decided he would become a world-famous dancer—the first dancing dog to make it big.

Boris reveled in all the imagined glory that went along with being a celebrity. He got so excited by the idea alone that instead of ambling from place to place like a normal dog, he pranced wherever he went. Lifting his paws high from the ground, Boris hoped he would improve the leg muscles necessary to perform complicated dancing routines. His every spare second was spent whirling and twirling, swooping and sweeping.

Boris was so enthused by his prancing and dancing that he constantly searched for reflections in windows and mirrors that could give him a glimpse of his fancy moves. Boris knew that he had set an ambitious goal for himself. Becoming a world-famous dog dancer was not going to be easy, but Boris had no lack of confidence in himself. He figured he had the will and the skill he would need to achieve his plan.

The first step for Boris was to find the right teacher—a teacher who recognized his great talent and who would be willing to help him get to the top, and fast. One morning, when Boris was discussing his plans with Gabby, she said, "You should talk to Prudence. She has won many dance competitions."

Boris was delighted to discover that his neighbor, Prudence, was a dancing dog diva. It didn't take him long to realize that Prudence possessed a lot of talent behind the prim and proper way she presented herself. Prudence took great interest in Boris, who was enthusiastic and naturally spry, and she taught him all of her favorite moves. She especially liked the one-legged hop and the two-paw bounce.

Boris quickly learned those moves, and his imagination and ego soared. He pictured himself on TV being praised as the greatest new canine sensation. He got excited just thinking about the fame and glory that would soon be his. After all, Liam and Aidan wildly applauded him for his clever dancing routines after dinner every night. In fact, Boris had quickly become the star of his neighborhood. People and pets would flock to Prudence's house just to watch him practice. Clearly, he felt like his plan was on track. It was only a matter of time before someone discovered his superior talent.

After several months, Prudence felt that Boris had mastered most of the difficult steps that she was able to teach him. She suggested that he enroll in a special camp designed to help highly talented dogs from all over the world learn the advanced skills required for stardom. Boris jumped at the opportunity. In fact, he had to make several figure-eight sprints around the yard to express his enthusiasm upon hearing about the camp. Before he could make ten twirling pirouettes, the Hamms had enrolled him in Camp Interbarkem.

At Interbarkem, Boris was surprised to find out that there were hundreds of very talented and frisky dogs like himself. Seeing the competition, he was forced to realize that his plan might not be as easy to accomplish as he had once thought. But this sobering experience made Boris work even harder. He practiced his clever routines several hours every day. Boris was determined to make his plan work. He was capable and committed, and he still believed that his dream was possible.

After many months of diligent practice, Boris heard news of a competition where he would be able to showcase his latest move, a creation of his very own: a whirling spin with ears pinned back and tail flopping in the breeze. This competition took place but once a year in Lansing, the state capital. Dogs from all over Michigan practiced for months to refine their skills. It was a major event that news media eagerly covered every year. This was Boris's big chance.

When the day of the competition arrived, Boris was feeling nervous. His paws grew sweaty as he waited for his opportunity to shine. Finally, it was time for him to perform. He took the stage and threw himself into his act. Boris whirled and twirled, dancing and prancing, flipping and dipping. His floppy ears were pinned to his head, and his tail was flowing beautifully. When he finished his routine, Boris was happy with his performance, so he felt quite certain that he would be crowned champion.

Unfortunately for Boris, the judges preferred another dog, named Twyla. Like Boris, Twyla was very talented. She was also perky and cute.

She smiled prettily at the judges as they rated her performance. Twyla had a beautiful, pointy nose and a tail that formed perfect curls. Her coat was perfectly groomed, and she wore red ribbons in her hair. To top it all off, he was even wearing a most stylish bonnet. Twyla was declared champion of the competition.

Boris was angry because he felt he had been cheated and that the scoring system was unfair. He felt he was every bit as talented as Twyla, and he wondered if she had even choreographed her own routine. "The judges must have favored Twyla because of her costume!" Boris thought huffily.

He felt he should have been judged solely on talent, not appearance. Besides, he believed that Twyla was more interested in pleasing the judges than challenging herself. She had danced flawlessly, but without much feeling, it seemed to Boris. She hadn't even taken any risks in her performance.

Boris snuck over to a corner of the tent where he could nurse his disappointment and gather strength to offer Twyla his congratulations. After ten minutes of sulking, his disappointment had settled down a bit. Once he had cooled down and was able to see the situation a little more clearly and objectively, Boris acknowledged that Twyla was very capable. While she might have played up to the judges, she had delivered a captivating performance, as well. Still, Boris just couldn't figure out what went into the judges' decision. He was thrown for a loop—but not a dancing loop.

A while later, Boris was still feeling really sorry for himself, convinced that life would be nothing without this victory to launch him into his inevitable rise to stardom. Then Prudence found him sitting by himself behind the bleachers. "I'll never make it big," Boris muttered to his teacher.

Prudence offered appropriate condolences and responded to the disappointment that Boris felt. She assured him he had done a wonderful job and that he should be proud of his performance. But then, as every great teacher does, Prudence challenged her student: "Boris, you need to take a hard look at what happened here. I'm not sure the conclusion you've come to is going to help you at all. If you want to win the next dance contest, you need to use this experience as a way to learn more about yourself and more about how the world really works. Your performance was excellent, but great performances don't always result in a win."

Boris was a bit taken aback by Prudence's comments. He was expecting to be petted and fed extra dog food—maybe even a biscuit. In fact, Boris was secretly hoping for a big pity party with lots of servings of sympathy. But upon hearing her words, he knew Prudence was right. He was glad he had chosen her as a teacher, not only because she had taught him terrific dance moves, but also because she didn't sugarcoat the truth.

Boris started to wonder, "Maybe the road to stardom is more complex than I had thought." He realized he appreciated Prudence's honesty and firmness as much as, if not more than, her support. Without her direct feedback, Boris wouldn't have the information he needed to make a good decision on what to do next. Boris had a lot of thinking to do about how much he was willing to work to achieve his dreams and how open he was to the feedback he would need to make improvements in his dancing skills.

Guide for Chapter 7:

▼

Boris Contemplates Freedom

In this story, Boris deals with the question of what it means to be free. The chapter confronts the issue of how we are all more conditioned by the culture in which we live than we often realize.

In preparation for this conversation, ask yourself how constrained you are by your environment and what price you are willing to pay for your freedom. How freely do you speak up when you have an opinion?

This story deals with freedom on multiple levels:

➢ Freedom to be who you are

➢ Freedom to think what you want to think

➢ Freedom to say what you want to say

➢ Freedom to explore any feelings you may have

➢ Freedom to act how you want to act

➢ Freedom from expectations

In my experience, the last two issues are tricky, because actions need to be socially responsible, and we are never free from certain expectations and obligations. The question is, how can we be free as individuals and still have a sense of order in our communities?

As a result of responding to this story, you might find yourself engaged with the child in any or all of these questions:

- Are there times when you have to pretend to be someone you're not?

- What, if anything, keeps you from exploring issues, ideas, feelings, and thoughts you might have?

- Have you ever had to keep your mouth shut when you really wanted to express your opinion?

- Are you doing what you want to be doing in life? Are you acting in ways that are consistent with what's most important to you?

- Are people expecting too much from you? Too little?

- Do you have to earn freedom? How do you do that?

CHAPTER 7

▼

BORIS CONTEMPLATES FREEDOM

Boris loved to listen to music. There was nothing he enjoyed more than putting on his ear phones and listening to the iPod that Liam and Aidan had bought him for his first anniversary with their family. Boris caused a lot of commotion in the neighborhood because he loved to dance on top of his doghouse when he listened to music. He would shake his whole body, turn flips, and keep time with the music with his head and tail wagging and flopping at the same time. Being free meant not being overly concerned about what other dogs thought about his funky moves. Seeing the other dogs snickering at him did not deter Boris from dancing with all of his heart and soul.

For some reason, Boris couldn't get enough of the lyrics in a song about getting free. The song went like this:

Just run in the rain, Jane.
Play in the snow, Flo.
You don't need to be smart, Art.
Just make yourself free.
Jump in the car, Gar.
You don't need to say much.
Put a note in the mail, Gail.
And make yourself free.

As Boris grew more responsible and had earned the Hamms' trust, they relaxed the rules they had imposed when he was a puppy. This song made

Boris think about how free he really was, though. He had learned how to channel his boundless energy into dancing and playing—when the time was right. He was also no longer confined to a cage at night.

Boris didn't feel like he had to act like most dogs or even think like most dogs. For that matter, Boris didn't even relate to other dogs like he was expected to as a normal dog in the neighborhood. The expectation for most dogs was to eat what they were served, sleep most of the day, and do their business outside. Nothing else was expected of them. But Boris liked to dance, form clubs, and engage in deep conversations with Zelda, as well.

Boris didn't like to fight, he didn't get jealous of other dogs (at least, not too often), and he enjoyed just hanging out and having a good time. And yet, he didn't really feel free. Although he was free to choose where to sleep in the house, the house was the limit. He couldn't sleep in the forest whenever he felt like watching the moon.

So what was freedom, really? Did it mean having no rules or chains? Did it mean being able to think what he wanted and to say what was on his mind? Or did it mean being able to create new visions of what might be possible for dogs in this world?

Boris knew one thing was for sure: freedom didn't mean the ability to say or do hateful things to his fellow dogs or to people. Thinking back on the song he liked so much, Boris decided he would make himself free. He didn't want to just run in the rain, play in the snow, or jump in the car; Boris wanted to get himself truly free.

He decided he would start by considering how free he was now. Questions popped into Boris's head wherever he went. When he was romping through the woods, he asked himself: "Which dogs do I talk to that make me think?" As he was chewing on his bone, another question interrupted his slurping and grinding: "Who do I ask for opinions about my ideas?" When he was hanging out with Lucky watching butterflies, another question barged in on his reverie: "Are there things I do simply because of what others expect dogs to do?" Boris couldn't even take a nap on his front porch without his active mind nagging him: "Am I really thinking of new possibilities for my life, or am I just choosing within the limited options that currently exist for dogs?"

Boris felt a little discouraged after he considered the choices he was asked to make in his daily life. He was surprised to discover that he had let other dogs think for him and that many of his actions, like barking at squirrels, were just a result of how dogs were expected to act in his neighborhood. This sudden realization gave Boris a jolt. In fact, the jolt was so strong that his headphones popped off his head and his iPod shut down.

Without the music blasting in his furry ears, Boris decided he would take a minute to think about the kind of song *he* would write about getting himself free. Here is what he came up with:

> Just create a new way, Ray.
> Have your own go, Moe.
> You can be smart, Art.
> Just think yourself free.
> Nest your idea, Leah.
> Find a new goal, Sol.
> Act on the facts, Max.
> Just think yourself free.

Boris felt the energy surge in his paws. He quickly put his headphones back on and cranked up his iPod. Before long, he was back up on his doghouse dancing and prancing. The neighbors shook their heads and said, "What a crazy dog."

But Boris didn't mind. He just shook his tail gleefully and shouted, "It's good to be free!"

GUIDE FOR CHAPTER 8:

▼

BORIS CONNECTS TO A HIGHER PURPOSE

In this story, Boris is searching for meaning in his life. He is looking for a way to get engaged in a project that is aligned with his quest to become the best dog he can be and to connect to his higher purpose.

In preparation for this conversation, think about the times in your life when you were most energized. Were you working on an important project, engaged in a stimulating relationship, or making progress on a personal goal?

There are several difficult challenges in this story. Finding a real purpose in life usually involves getting outside oneself and helping others. Staying focused on that purpose requires real commitment and capability. Developing that capability encompasses several skills. These five skills all play a role in finding meaning in our lives:

➤ Defining a mission outside oneself

➤ Brainstorming possibilities

➤ Finding meaningful work

➤ Promoting an idea

➤ Sustaining change

In my experience as a person committed to personal development, my first step was to find a higher purpose. The purpose I chose was creating healthy, innovative, and productive environments. I tried working in jails, social service agencies, schools, hospitals, and corporations. In each setting, I documented what I learned and made it available to others.

As a result of responding to this story, you might find yourself engaged with the child in any or all of these questions:

- What, in life, gives you the most satisfaction?

- When do you feel really good about what you're doing and how you spend your time?

- What is the best idea you ever had, and how did you share that idea with your friends?

- What makes it so hard to behave in ways that are consistent with what you believe is most important?

- Which of your friends seem the most self-absorbed or self-centered?

- What happens when you introduce a new idea to your friends? Do they think of ways to make the idea better or just tell you why the idea won't work?

CHAPTER 8

▼

BORIS CONNECTS TO A HIGHER PURPOSE

Boris felt lost. He found he was spending a lot of time just wandering around the backyard feeling sorry for himself. He had been with the Hamm fam for almost two years now, and his life had settled into a predictable routine. He was worried that his quest for an extraordinary life was losing steam. His tail would drag on the ground, his chin hanging down and his ears flat as he walked. Instead of prancing and dancing, Boris was stooping and drooping.

One day Boris decided to go looking for company. Maybe playing with his neighborhood friends would lift his spirits. As he left his backyard, he saw a pack of his pals hanging around on the corner.

"What's up?" Boris asked as he approached them. He wagged his tail to indicate that he was happy to see them.

Prudence responded, "We were just complaining about how there's nothing to do."

"Yeah. We're boooored," sighed Lucky.

"Maybe we can find a project or a game to occupy our time," Boris suggested.

Prudence threw out an idea. "Maybe we can solve world hunger for dogs!"

All of them fell to the ground laughing at that idea—it was way too big to even consider. Then Sally Siamese added an idea to the mix: "How about if we create a gallery for animal art?"

Gabby said, "Yeah, right. You're the only animal artist I know."

Lucky scratched his chin with his paw and thought about the boy in his house who was having trouble reading. Suddenly he barked out, "We could teach kids to read!"

The other dogs rolled on the ground, howling at what a stupid idea that was. But Boris remembered how Liam loved to read to him. For some reason, Liam felt safe and comfortable reading to Boris, but he had trouble reading in front of adults or other children. "Boris, come here and sit next to me while I read," Liam would often say. "I know you won't correct my mistakes, and you always perk up your ears when I read to you."

Boris shared these facts with the others, and this made the other dogs think. They could all remember times when children had confided in them, even though the children didn't think the dogs really understood them. Of course, they were wrong about that.

Boris, Lucky, and Prudence grew excited about the possibilities of helping children read, but they couldn't figure out how to show their grown-up human friends that they could really make a difference. They decided the best thing to do was to keep their ears up and their eyes open for chances to snuggle up to children whenever they happened to be reading.

They put their plan into action. At first, they noticed that when they sat next to children and looked at them, the children seemed happier to be reading. The dogs knew that they couldn't act eager to play, because that would distract the child. They found that if they calmly settled down next to a child who was reading, the child would keep on reading, seeming to relax and to enjoy the book. Boris was able to sit quietly while Liam read to him, even though he found this particularly difficult because he loved to wiggle. Sitting still was not Boris's specialty.

Little by little, parents started noticing that their children were not only spending more time reading, but they also seemed to be having fun and learning more. Their grades even started improving. The parents could not figure out what had happened until Grandfather Bob remarked to Mr. and Mrs. Hamm, "Have you noticed that the more Boris hangs out with Liam, the more he reads?"

When Bob shared this observation with other parents, they all agreed that every dog in the neighborhood seemed to be keenly attentive whenever children were reading. Even Sally and some of the other neighborhood cats would curl up near a reading child now and then and just purr. Boris and his friends were very pleased that the parents saw the value in what the dogs and cats were doing. Boris became so fired up that he started recruiting dogs from other neighborhoods to help with his mission. Not only did the pets feel terrific because they were helping the people they loved the most, but they also realized they were no longer bored.

Boris had regained zest for his quest. He had found something meaningful and satisfying to do with his free time.

GUIDE FOR CHAPTER 9:

▼

BORIS RECALLS HIS EARLY PUPPYHOOD

In this story, Boris's finely tuned senses bring back joyful memories of when he was a new puppy in his original home.

In preparation for this conversation, reflect upon which sense or senses trigger the most memories for you.

This story contains several potentially divergent paths to conversation:

➢ Recalling memories

➢ Defining the simple principles of life

➢ Giving love freely

➢ Using all the senses to find joy

➢ Resolving unanswered questions

I grew up next door to legendary football coach Jack Streidl and his family—his extraordinary wife, Phyllis, plus their eight wonderful children. I remember fondly the texture of the rope we would use to swing from roof to roof, the smells of all the animals (snakes, squirrels, turtles, monkeys, parrots, dogs) we captured or collected to play with for a while, and the sounds of all the children playing kickball, football, basketball, or any sport other sport we invented for the day.

As a result of responding to this story, you might find yourself engaged with the child in any or all of these questions:

- What are a few of your happiest memories?

- Which simple ideas or values did you learn when you were little that still hold true now that you're older?

- Who have you known who has loved those around them freely and given generously?

- Which senses trigger the most memories for you?

- Why do some people act so differently from one day to another? For example, why are some friends nice to you one day, but maybe mean to you another?

CHAPTER 9

▼

BORIS RECALLS HIS EARLY PUPPYHOOD

Boris sniffed and sniffed. Something smelled familiar; some wonderful smell triggered fond memories of his earlier days as a tiny puppy in the cozy living room of his first home. He moved, following the scent of the sweet smell, and sniffed some more. His nose scrunched up, his eyes got wider, and his tail wagged as he drifted off into the sweet memory of his six brothers and sisters nudging up against one another next to their mother.

Boris had forgotten those carefree days of playful pouncing, bravado barking, and harmless nipping that had filled his early puppyhood days. Now, due to this smell, he began to recreate the memories of careless cavorting around the kitchen with his equally rambunctious brothers and sisters. Life was so simple then: suck gently and play hard. If you tried to take more than your share, you got a firm push from your mother's paw. If playing hard turned to playing mean, your brothers and sisters gave you a sharp rebuke, like a scrunched-up forehead and a mean glare.

Boris finally remembered the source of the sweet smell that triggered these memories. His first human family consisted of a warm, friendly woman with three children. She simply loved freely. Boris and his brothers and sisters gave her endless delight, and she seemed to have a boundless supply of caresses, pets, pats, and strokes—and sometimes special treats to brighten their day and please their palates.

The most sumptuous odors emanated from her kitchen throughout the day. In the morning, Boris loved the smell of fried bacon and eggs, even though he was perfectly content with his mother's milk. At noon, his owner would bake corn fritters with thick molasses syrup that made Boris's mouth water, even though he only tasted it once—one day, she had let Boris lick her finger after cooking, and new worlds opened up in his mind. At night, smells of beef and broccoli wafted from the kitchen. Boris's favorite, though, was the aroma of the angel food cake prepared with his owner's special orange sauce. Boris was now catching a whiff of orange.

"Ahh," Boris thought, "how a smell can take you back and make you smile. I do so love that smell and the memories it brings." The memories took him away from the troubling thoughts of adjustment, anticipation, and anxiety he had occasionally experienced since starting a new life on his own.

Boris wondered if he would ever be reunited with his mother, brothers, and sisters. And he still didn't quite understand how the kind woman who had raised his mother and given him treats could have just dropped him off on the road when he was still a puppy. All he knew was that he needed to keep growing as an individual so that he could feel good about his own life make his mother proud.

GUIDE FOR CHAPTER 10:

▼

BORIS CLEARS HIS MIND AND THINKS POSITIVELY

In this story, Boris learns the power of meditation. He finds out there is a way to catch yourself being negative and to find a new, positive energy.

In preparation for this conversation, ask yourself how much energy you waste with negative emotions. What causes you to slip into a negative state? How well do you notice yourself falling into that state, and how do you get yourself out of it?

This story contains many spiritual exercises essential to growth:

➢ Being grateful for every day we are given

➢ Confronting negative behavior

➢ Thinking positively

➢ Meditating peacefully

➢ Living in the world, but not being of the world

In my experience, it is easy to find excuses and distractions for not doing the work required to clear one's mind. It's hard to maintain an attitude toward life that each day is a bonus and that it's important to rejoice in every day we have been given. Seeing each day as an opportunity to make progress and grow is a critical first step, but there are many obstacles to throw a person off his or her quest: slipping into negative thoughts, feelings, and behaviors;

getting caught up in the culture in which we live, learn, and work; and giving in to primal instincts.

As a result of responding to this story, you might find yourself engaged with the child in any or all of these questions:

- What do you do when you get in a negative mood?

- How do you think meditation exercises might help you?

- How can we live in the world but not get caught up in activities that are unhealthy or don't make us feel good about ourselves?

- Is there anything that keeps you from doing what you really want to do? If so, what is it, and how can you get around that?

Chapter 10

▼

Boris Clears His Mind and Thinks Positively

Boris was grumpy over the terrible weather. It was the fiftieth day of a heat wave. Boris had just celebrated his second anniversary with the Hamm fam, and he couldn't believe how fast time had flown.

On this hot day, Boris was carrying on to Zelda about how much he hated the heat and how the high humidity made him miserable. "If only it was seventy degrees and sunny every day, I could be happy," moaned Boris. It was a big joke in the neighborhood that Boris had to check the weather report before he could tell you how he was feeling.

Zelda had listened to his complaining for what seemed like hours when finally she said to Boris, "This is the day we have been given; rejoice and grow in it."

Boris was shocked at Zelda's direct encouragement to take what the day gives you and make the most of it. She was usually more patient and supportive, rather than blunt. Boris had heard the saying, "This is the day we have been given; rejoice and be glad in it," but he hadn't heard the statement end in "grow in it." He asked Zelda what she meant by that.

Zelda responded, "Look, Boris, we have so many things to be thankful for. We need to take the focus away from our negative thoughts and shift it toward more productive thoughts. I have found that reciting a simple meditation helps me calm my thoughts and feel more together."

She then shared with Boris a meditation she used to clear her mind and to prepare herself for any opportunity that might come along. This is what she said:

I am at one.
I am at peace.
I am calm and still.
I am here now.
I can lighten up.
I can be kind.
I can extend love.
I can smile on the world.
I wish I were more awake.
I wish I were more unified.
I wish I could be of more help.
I am like a big mountain.
I am like a warm sea.
I am like a free flower.
I am thankful for the earth and my body.
I am thankful for water and my soul.
I am thankful for the sun and for fire.
I am thankful for the air and my spirit.
I am thankful for beautiful sounds.
I am thankful to be loved.
I am thankful to have hope.
I am thankful for my senses.
I will try to be who I am.
I will try to be honest.
I will try to listen to nature.
I will try to connect to a higher purpose.
I will try to send positive energy into my world.

Boris wasn't quite sure what to say after Zelda completed the meditation. He had never tried to clear his mind in that way. He had never tried to give thanks for all the things he took for granted, either.

After he spent some time thinking, Boris responded to Zelda, "I'm not sure I could say or do all those things. They seem so simple on the one hand, and so hard on the other. It sounds like something a dog might say if he went off to live in a cave for a year. How can I learn to stay calm and still hang out in the neighborhood with my friends?"

"You don't need to run off to a cave," Zelda assured Boris. "You just need to find time each day to relax and give thanks. Maybe you would feel more positive about today if we went for a swim. You can be thankful for the water and for the chance to cool down."

Boris and Zelda sprinted down to the lake and plunged right into the waves without even slowing down. They splashed each other, shook water all over the sunbathers lying on the beach, and then dove right back into the lake for another swim. Boris celebrated how cool he felt. He wasn't yet sure how he was going to use the rest of the day he had been given, but he was definitely feeling more positive.

GUIDE FOR CHAPTER 11:

▼

BORIS HELPS CREATE PEACE

In this story, Boris tries to find peaceful solutions to ongoing conflicts and at the same time figure out how to deal with the bullies on the block: in this case, the mean dogs and rogue packs.

As you prepare for this conversation, think about the roles, religion, ethnic group, political party, nation, or region with which you strongly identify. Ask yourself how those identifications have influenced your belief system and have led you to draw conclusions or to act in ways that you later regretted.

This story highlights several of the roadblocks to finding peaceful solutions:

➤ Overidentifying

➤ Imposing one's own point of view

➤ Seeing differences as problems instead of as gifts

➤ Relying on the same old responses, leading to the same, negative outcomes

The story also alludes to important skills that could play a role in producing positive, sustainable outcomes:

➤ Resisting cultural norms (that is, dealing with peer pressure)

➤ Innovating and staying open to nontraditional or unconventional ideas

➤ Finding healthy exceptions to the rules

In my experience as a parent, I have found that children need to learn all of these skills. Peer pressure exerts an enormous influence on children's behavior, and they need to find ways to "get away clean"—which is to say, how to resist peer pressure from friends who want them to do something they really don't want to do, but in a way that doesn't alienate the friends.

I encouraged my children to be open to exploring unconventional choices and to consider a range of possibilities that could result in a transformative experience. I would help them find healthy exceptions to traditional problem resolution and find positive role models, like leaders who were able to find diplomatic solutions to conflicts. I asked them to consider why one person might succeed where others did not.

As a result of responding to this story, you might find yourself engaged with the child in any or all of these questions:

- Have you ever had to deal with a bully? What did you do?

- What roles do you identify with? For example, do you identify as a student, as an athlete, as a person from a particular gender, age, or race?

- Which of your friends are really different from you, and what have you learned from them as a result of these differences?

CHAPTER 11

▼

BORIS HELPS CREATE PEACE

Boris was worried. All the dogs in the nearby neighborhoods had formed packs that were constantly fighting each other. Just last week, Lucky suffered a nasty bite from a dog in one of the packs, even though he hadn't been involved in their conflicts. Lucky had just been peacefully strolling down the road when four dogs jumped out of the trees. They surrounded him, threatened to take his collar, and then one of the meaner members nipped Lucky's leg before the gang scampered away. Boris remembered that Lucky had warned him about packs like these the first week he had arrived at the Hamm house.

Boris did not see himself as a member of any pack. He had problems even seeing himself as just a dog, so he couldn't understand why these dogs were always fighting with each other. He learned that once a dog joined a pack, the dog was expected to stay close to that pack. And every pack had its own code of behavior that separated it from the others. The mongrel pack would bare their teeth and growl at any strange dog that happened to wander into their territory. The purebred pack dedicated themselves to strutting around, showing their superiority and making grand displays of tail wagging and barking. The show dog pack spent most of their days coming up with ways to show off their refinement and talents.

Every week, these packs would run into each other and get into big fights. One pack might scare away a neighboring pack on Tuesday, but they would suffer humiliation and defeat on Wednesday. And then, of course, there were random acts of meanness like the one that Lucky experienced.

Boris tried and tried to come up with a solution for bringing all the dogs together, but nothing he could imagine gave him much hope. He decided to visit Zelda. Boris knew that Zelda would not suggest an easy or typical solution—she didn't like the "conventional," as she called it. She preferred more innovative ideas. That meant that, like Boris, she loved to think about new ways of doing things. She always tried to come up with creative ideas and give them voice. Many times, Zelda's ideas were rejected by those who preferred traditional approaches. Boris knew, however, that the solution for this sticky problem wouldn't come from ordinary discussions with ordinary dogs.

As Boris had hoped, Zelda came up with some great ideas. "Boris, what if you paid a visit to each pack and asked if they *liked* constantly fighting and being trapped in one group," she suggested. "You might also ask them if they know of any packs who are getting along and what makes that possible."

Zelda knew there was no magic to these solutions, but she also knew that it was the only place to start—to ask each pack to come up with their own solutions. What made Zelda's idea unique was, her plan started with asking questions, rather than telling others what to do.

Boris decided to give Zelda's idea a try. He found a hat that he thought made him look diplomatic and a white flag to carry in his mouth when he visited each group. The diplomatic hat was a tall, black head covering from which Boris's ears stuck out, making him look a little silly. The white flag was meant to communicate that Boris came in peace with no ill intentions.

Fortunately, after having spent almost three years with the Hamm fam, Boris was well-known around town. His love for exploring had led him to meet new dogs in several other neighborhoods. Therefore, all the packs knew that Boris wasn't a member of any rival pack—for, as we know, Boris didn't identify himself with any group at all. So when Boris showed up in each neighborhood, he was welcomed as a dog who came in peace. The way he wagged his tail, bobbed his head, and pranced through the streets didn't hurt, either.

As he went from pack to pack, Boris kept on the lookout for the rogue gang that had ambushed Lucky. Maybe he could discover their reasons for their behavior. But his main mission was to ask each pack the questions that Zelda had suggested.

Boris polled the mongrels, the purebreds, and the show dogs about why all the groups of dogs were fighting. Every dog was happy to give their answers—after all, it wasn't often that they were asked what they thought, instead of told what to think by other dogs who thought they were right.

The mongrel pack said to Boris, "The other packs are always calling us low-class mutts. They say our inferior breeding doesn't give us the right to travel in their circles."

The purebred pack had a different story to tell. "We're tired of other dogs thinking we're stuck-up brats. They say our beautiful fur coats make them sick."

The show dog pack shared their recent experience with a pack of dogs that seemed to get along well with other dogs and seemed to spend their entire day playing games and having fun. "When we wandered into their territory, they wagged their tails, licked our faces, and invited us to join in their games. When we asked them how they were able to avoid fighting and bickering with other groups, they replied, 'Because we care less about our differences than what we have in common.'"

After a good deal of discussion, with Boris as the diplomat, each of the three packs decided that things weren't going exactly the way they had hoped. They all knew of other packs who managed to get along, so maybe, they decided that they were sick of bickering with each other over their differences. They realized that they didn't need to have enemies, and they were sick of living in fear. They all realized they had been fighting just for the sake of fighting—nothing else.

Boris trotted happily back to Zelda to tell her the news. Zelda was pleased that Boris's conversations had gone well. But she advised Boris not to fool himself by thinking that the problem was solved. She said, in her experience, that the only way to end fighting was to make sure all the leaders of the packs remained committed to peace. And then there was always the nasty problem of what to do with the other bullies on the block—the rogues. Boris was pleased with his progress, but he knew there was a lot more work to do.

GUIDE FOR CHAPTER 12:

▼

BORIS DISCOVERS THE PROBLEM WITH RELATIONSHIPS

In this story, Boris has a misunderstanding with one of his best friends. He tries to figure out the root cause of the problem.

In preparation for this conversation, think about which of your friends you have the most fun with. Which ones introduce you to new ideas and new adventures?

This story encompasses many factors in healthy relationships. In relationships that contribute to spiritual health, these behaviors and attitudes usually exist:

➢ Being open to new adventures

➢ Looking beyond idiosyncrasies

➢ Sharing decision making

➢ Agreeing on truth and blame

In my experience, the relationships I value most are with people who may have off-putting behaviors, but who have real depth and substance. They tend to be people who don't follow the crowd and who are not totally driven by materialism. I find it easy in these relationships to share ideas and to reach agreement on cause and effect. At a minimum, I can respect their points of view, even if I disagree with them from time to time.

As a result of responding to this story, you might find yourself engaged with the child in any or all of these questions:

- Have you ever had a falling out with a friend? What caused it?

- Do you have friends with irritating habits that you are able to ignore because you care about them so much?

- With which people in your life do you have the most trouble reaching agreement on what's right and what's wrong? Who is at fault when things go wrong? Who, if anyone, is blamed?

CHAPTER 12

▼

BORIS DISCOVERS THE PROBLEM WITH RELATIONSHIPS

Boris was sad. He and Sally Siamese had played together for months and had been friends for a long time, so their fight today came as a big blow to Boris.

Boris enjoyed Sally because she was a very smart cat and was constantly opening up new ideas and ways of thinking that he would have never discovered on his own. For instance, Sally loved to find tasty berries in the woods and share them with Boris. To her, the outdoors was like a free store where you could find anything you could possibly want—all you had to do was look. She found scrumptious mushrooms, fragrant flowers, and an occasional mouse—though Sally always pouted when Boris turned down Sally's generous offer to share a bowl of mouse mousse.

Sally was quick and agile. She would jump from table to table or limb to limb without the slightest effort. She moved silently and swiftly through the woods so that none of the animals would suspect her presence unless she wanted them to. Daydreaming mice had no chance with Sally. Sometimes even an especially meaty bird would fall prey to her hunting skills.

What Sally loved most of all was to draw pictures in the sand on the beach. She would spend hours thinking about each line and shape. Then before long, a wave would come and wash away her long-thought-over drawing. Her friends didn't understand. Almost in a chorus, they would say, "Sally, why don't you put your drawings on paper and sell them? You could make a lot of money."

Sally responded indignantly, "I don't draw for dollars. I create to capture my understanding of a moment." Her friends would roll their eyes, twitch their whiskers, and shake their heads.

Boris appreciated Sally's dedication and her commitment to leading a different kind of life. She certainly wasn't like any of the dogs he knew. She wasn't even like most of the cats he knew. Sally wasn't interested in joining catty cat clubs. She just wanted to live an independent life and to make art.

Boris's tail would always wag when he saw Sally slipping into his yard with her penetrating eyes. He knew that Sally picked up on every cue—from the smallest breaking twig to the heavy breathing of a not-so-friendly dog. She was always a little guarded because she wasn't sure that dogs, even Boris, really understood her. But Boris loved Sally so much that he didn't let her moodiness or distance put him off.

One day when Sally came over, Boris said, "Today we'll play any game you choose to play."

Sally was thrilled. She wrinkled her brow and flicked her ears back and forth. She pushed her lips out and made her whiskers move up and down, which let Boris know she was giving a lot of thought to this decision. Finally, she decided that they would go on a mushroom hunt. Upon saying this, she noticed that Boris's ears dropped and his head sank slightly lower.

"Okay, what's up, Boris?" Sally asked.

Boris admitted that he had just been out in the woods yesterday with Lucky and Gabby searching for those ever-elusive mushrooms that everyone seemed so wild about. Sensing Sally's disappointment, he asked her about several other possibilities he thought she might like. "What about looking for berries? Or how about if we go down to the beach and draw pictures in the sand? Have you thought about sneaking up on birds? Why don't you understand that I would rather do something else today?"

Boris's barrage of questions irritated Sally. She hated questions, particularly when they never seemed to end. In response, she simply turned and slinked away.

Boris was crushed. When he followed her and asked her what was the matter, she told him she felt misunderstood and was uncomfortable hanging out with him. Boris's head jerked back, and his jaw dropped open. He couldn't believe their friendship could change so quickly.

Boris dragged his tail out to the pond in search of Zelda. The trip took an especially long time, because each step was a struggle. He just plodded away, one paw ahead of the other. Not a single hair stood up on his back, and an occasional tear dripped from his eyes, ran down his nose, and dropped to the ground.

Boris was relieved to find Zelda at home. She listened intently as Boris shared his story. Zelda finally said, "Boris, cats and dogs have different ideas about what is true and who is at fault—that's why different individuals sometimes misunderstand or misinterpret each other. It sounds like Sally just can't believe you totally accept her and love her, even though you have had so many wonderful moments together. In this case, maybe Sally believes you thought she has bad ideas, while you believe you were just trying to be helpful. Plus, she's mad because you changed the rules of the game. She understood that she could choose the game of the day because you said she could, but then you started suggesting your own ideas. From your point of view, you didn't see yourself as trying to get your way, and you believed she still knew the decision was hers."

Boris nodded his head slowly. As he plodded his way back to the Hamm house, he realized Zelda was right. Friends have different views of how things go down, and sometimes it's very hard to work through them.

GUIDE FOR CHAPTER 13:

▼

BORIS MANAGES
HIS IMPULSES

In this story, Boris struggles with how to deal with his primary instincts. He tries to understand which ones to free and which ones to restrain.

In preparation for your conversation, think about how basic instincts might have caused you problems in the past.

The key question in this story is, who's driving your life? The story addresses critical challenges faced on the quest for unity and growth:

➢ Closing down primal instincts

➢ Dealing with hormonal changes

➢ Observing your thoughts and feelings

➢ Choosing how to act on those thoughts and feelings

➢ Listening to your conscience

In my experience, I have found it difficult to keep a constant watch on my thoughts and feelings so that I could make more thoughtful and conscious decisions on how to act. Over the past twenty years, I have practiced a healing form of tai chi, which is simply a series of exercises consisting of slow, conscious movements. These exercises have helped remind me to close down my primal instincts. As I breathe in during certain movements, I say, "Close the primal." As I breathe out, I say, "Open the possible." Doing these exercises over a long period of time has given me a better sense of control; it has helped me manage my tendencies to be competitive and aggressive. I feel like I'm more in charge of my own destiny because of tai chi.

As a result of responding to this story, you might find yourself engaged with the child in any or all of these questions:

- Have your impulses caused you problems before? What impulses?

- Have you ever found you were reacting without thinking? Could that have led to a negative consequence?

- Have you ever had a really negative thought or feeling that you were able to identify, allowing you to make a constructive choice instead of an impulsive one?

CHAPTER 13

▼

BORIS MANAGES
HIS IMPULSES

Boris had just celebrated his fourth anniversary with the Hamm fam. He was surprised as he grew older how his body went through so many changes—even his feelings and moods seemed to change.

Boris felt especially puzzled by his instincts—feelings of competitiveness and aggression. These feelings sometimes led to trouble. On the one paw, they seemed so natural. On the other paw, acting on them sometimes got him in trouble. If another dog barked at him, he wanted to bark right back. If he visited a doghouse that was bigger than his, he wanted it and he hated the dog who lived there (at least for a flashing instant). If he saw a dog with a fine coat of hair, he got insanely jealous. He might mope around the house for a week if that coat was really shiny and soft. If he saw owners pet their dog affectionately, he whined horribly until someone petted him, too. If he saw a beautiful female dog, he wanted to go right up to her and rub noses or smell her. It was a constant struggle for Boris to know which instincts to act on and which ones to just observe and let go.

Boris didn't share these secret thoughts with anyone, but the thoughts worried him every day. What Boris didn't know was that other dogs would have known exactly what he was feeling—they all dealt with similar types of instincts. But Boris was upset about these instincts because he saw himself as a thoughtful, kind, and compassionate dog. And, in fact, he was.

One day, when his secret thoughts were really bugging him, Boris happened to run into Zelda. Over the years, he had come to trust Zelda very deeply. They had had many conversations over that time, and Boris always valued Zelda's wise counsel. He decided to share what was bothering him.

Zelda listened carefully to Boris and then said, "You know, Boris, all dogs have secret thoughts and feelings, but most are not aware of what those feelings are or how they lead to behaviors that get them into trouble. More importantly, most dogs act on those thoughts and feelings without even giving it a thought. I admire you for being aware of those feelings, being willing to share them, and being able to make good choices about those feelings most of the time. It's okay to feel anything you feel, but it's not okay to act on everything you feel. Boris, you seem to manage your instincts well, and you exercise real restraint in how you act on certain instincts. But it's always a struggle to maintain that balance."

"What does restraint mean?" Boris asked.

Zelda explained, "Restraint means being able to identify a thought or feeling and make a wise choice about how to act on that feeling or thought."

Boris was relieved by what his friend had said. She reassured him that his thoughts and feelings were normal and that he was doing well in his efforts to manage them. After this talk with Zelda, he figured he would never feel conflicted again. He thought about one time he was so torn about what to do: should he snap at Sally for teasing him, or should he just laugh it off and have some fun? It seemed to him like choices like that would be easier to make now that he knew about impulses.

As Boris was prancing home in a much lighter mood, he saw Tom Terrier with a tasty-looking bone in his mouth. The first thought that popped into Boris's head was, "That bone looks delicious! I should snatch it away from Tom and take it home with me. I'm bigger and stronger than Tom is; it would be easy pickings."

But just as Boris took the first steps toward Tom, a voice inside him said, "Boris, you're not a greedy bully. Stop right where you are!"

Boris felt ashamed. He had felt much better after talking to Zelda and had promised himself he would try to control his feelings, but here he was already faced with a situation in which he had difficulty controlling himself.

It was then that Boris fully realized that this was a problem everyone probably faced, as Zelda had said. He was beginning to know the right thing to do without really thinking about it, but he knew he would still need to observe himself to make sure he was in control of his feelings. A thought popped into his mind: "Just because you *can* do something doesn't mean you *should*."

GUIDE FOR CHAPTER 14:

▼

BORIS EXPECTS BETTER FROM HIMSELF

In this story, Boris tries to improve his level of functioning in many ways: physically, emotionally, intellectually, and spiritually. He finds there are many pitfalls along the way, including his own self-deception.

In preparation for this conversation, reflect upon your attempts to become a more rounded person and to achieve a higher level wellness.

This story goes to the heart of human growth and development. There are several serious themes that play out in this silly episode with Boris:

➢ Seeking wholeness

➢ Making a strong effort

➢ Wishing versus working

➢ Assessing your abilities

In my experience, finding balance and wholeness is not an easy task. It takes constant effort. I have found that I tend to get lost in one dimension and lose track of the others. For example, I might spend so much time exercising that I don't pay enough attention to the people I love or become too tired to read the books I want to read.

In this society, I find that most people devote their time to pursuing intellectual or work objectives or to chasing physical and material goals. I have also observed that people who tend to act in ways that are outside the norms of the social groups in which they live can be ignored or excluded, even though they might have creative ideas or unique knowledge.

As a result of responding to this story, you might find yourself engaged with the child in any or all of these questions:

- What physical activity do you enjoy the most?

- What are your favorite books or movies?

- Who do you like to hang out with?

- Do you remember ever feeling really connected and at peace? When were those times?

- Why is it so hard to be healthy?

- What has been your experience when you have tried to excel, but your peer group distracted you? For example, have you ever wanted to do your homework, but your friends persuaded you to watch TV or go online instead?

CHAPTER 14

▼

BORIS EXPECTS BETTER FROM HIMSELF

There came a day when Boris expected better for himself. He wanted to become stronger, and he wanted to learn more about the world around him.

Boris thought it was going to be easy to improve himself in these ways. When he'd first started on this quest to lead a rich, full life over four years ago, he'd figured all he had to do was set a goal and make it happen. But Boris was surprised to find out that wishing to achieve a goal—like having strong muscles or being able to run faster—was far different than reaching it.

Boris thought a good place to start would be to get in shape. Lately he had been spending a lot of his time lying around on the porch or occasionally sneaking into the house to watch TV and eat snacks. He decided he was going to start running ten laps around his yard every morning, and he was going to stop eating treats the neighbors gave him when he wasn't hungry.

Boris got off to a terrific start. The first morning, he jumped out of bed, whined at the door until Mr. Hamm let him out, and immediately started running as fast as he could. Halfway through the first lap, Boris felt like a super-dog. For that first half lap, he moved so fast he looked like a blur. But three steps later, Boris was short of breath, and his legs were sore. By the end of the first lap, he was barely even jogging. He wondered how he was ever going to complete nine more laps.

Slowing down the pace seemed to help, and with great effort Boris completed the ten laps. Slowly, he huffed and puffed his way back to his favorite spot on the porch, where he collapsed in an exhausted heap. Though he was a little tired the rest of the day, he was proud of himself for his achievement. Boris did well on his exercise routine for the whole week, and he noticed by the end of it that the laps were easier to run. He had learned from the first day's effort that it was always wiser to start out a little slower and to end strong.

On the eighth day, however, Boris ran into an unexpected problem. The other dogs in the neighborhood came over and complained to him that their families were now pushing them to start exercising, as well! Prudence was especially upset. Her family, the Rohs, had started putting a leash around her neck and making her go for walks. All the dogs chimed in until there was a virtual chorus of complaints. Boris didn't want his friends to be angry with him; he wanted them to like him, so he stopped listening to his own thoughts and let his friends tell him what to do—he would not exercise so much when others were watching. Before long, his runs were fewer and farther between.

Instead, Boris shifted his energy to his learning goal. He went to the library and found several books he had wanted to read. When he checked them out, the librarian said, "Boris, aren't you biting off more than you can chew?" Then she started laughing. She thought it was funny that Boris was trying to act like a human, but he still had to carry the books in his mouth. Boris was not amused, though, because he thought the librarian was not taking his efforts to learn seriously. He took his books and trotted home, determined to meet his goals.

Boris decided that instead of running laps in the morning, he would do push-ups in his doghouse and then lie on the porch and read for an hour to start each day. He also decided he would limit himself to just fifteen minutes per day on his favorite Web site, www.doggie.com. Boris just loved to search the Internet for new doggie toys.

Sure enough, the next morning, Boris did fifty push-ups in his doghouse, then he grabbed his book and walked over to the front porch. After reading just one chapter, he was thoroughly captivated by the book. In fact, Boris was so lost in the story he didn't even notice when Lucky came over and sat down beside him. Lucky had to bark three times to get his attention. Startled at the sound, Boris leaped up. It took him a few moments to get reoriented to real life.

Lucky just shook his head and said, "You lead a strange life, Boris! If you're not running around the house trying to get in shape, you're reading a book on the porch. Can't you be an ordinary dog like the rest of us and just relax?"

Boris, a little embarrassed, replied, "I just like all these pictures." Then he said, "Hey, want to play a game?"

Lucky responded quickly, "Yeah! Come and chase some squirrels with me." Boris put down his book and loped off the porch with his friend Lucky.

That night, Boris felt mad at himself because he hadn't stuck to his plans. He had given up running because of pressure from his friends, and it seemed like there were always good reasons to do something other than read. He felt like a ball being thrown up in the air: the ball would quickly rise high into the air, then it would slow down and finally get pulled back to earth by a mysterious force (also known as gravity). Boris wanted to keep on rising—keep striving for his goals—but he knew, just like the ball, he would always have to deal with the forces that kept pulling him down, like the opinions of his friends. Meeting his own high standards did not seem to be getting any easier, even after four years on his quest.

GUIDE FOR CHAPTER 15:

▼

BORIS ADVOCATES
FOR GRATITUDE

In this story, Boris attempts to be more grateful for all the gifts that nature gives him each day. He finds that some friends would rather stew in their negative attitudes.

In preparation for this conversation, ask yourself how conscious you are of nature's constantly unfolding wonders. How aware are you of the world around you?

This story covers a few of life's blessings that Boris happens to notice. There are several generic themes, however, contained within the story:

➢ Being grateful

➢ Creating your own story

➢ Dealing with negativity

➢ Confronting victimhood

In my experience, I have benefited the most from people who were willing to shock my sense of self-satisfaction by confronting some of my negative behaviors. While I didn't appreciate the confrontations in the moment, I later realized that they jolted me into a more realistic picture of myself and motivated me to grow.

I discovered in my work with inmates that if I simply gave back to them in a paraphrased way what they were saying to me, they were left with their "emotional garbage" instead of getting me to carry it. For example, an inmate might say, "Those guards really suck. They're always pushing me around." A response might be, "You're angry because you are not being treated the way you would like to be treated." The inmate's anger would dissipate because he was being heard (though not necessarily agreed with). And then, having less anger, he might be able to ask himself *why* he was being treated in ways he didn't like.

If you are always taking on others' problems, you can quickly lose perspective on what's important. This attitude is not about being cavalier and unhelpful, it's about compassionately reframing what the other person says and letting them own it.

As a result of responding to this story, you might find yourself engaged with the child in any or all of these questions:

What are you most grateful for?

- How do you deal with people who are negative?

- Can you think of a time when someone has said something to you that shocked you into taking a hard look at yourself? Is that person still your friend?

- What kind of story are you creating with your own life?

Chapter 15

▼

Boris Advocates for Gratitude

Boris decided to keep a gratitude book to write down everything he was thankful for each day. For his first entry, he wrote this poem:

I stood in awe
Of everything I saw
Unfurl for me today.
The earth goes round the sun
I had lots of fun
My day was full of play.
There's so much to know
I have every chance to grow
And the stars twinkle in space.
I have a brain to think
My cheeks are very pink
And I have a sweet, brown face.
I still hope that life holds more
I can't guess what's still in store
But I'm amazed by life's mystery.
I can taste, touch, and feel.
I have a really good deal.
I feel lucky to make my history.

As Boris reflected on his poem, he felt full of gratitude. He was putting the final touches on his poem when Prudence strayed into his yard. Noticing Boris's state of bliss, she said, "What's up, Boris? You look mellow."

Boris replied, "I just made the first entry in my gratitude book, and I was feeling very thankful."

Prudence stuck up her tiny, pointy nose, flipped her curly ears over her head, and gave Boris a wide-eyed look of disbelief. She whined, "Thankful for what? *My* life is terrible. I stepped in a mud puddle and got my shiny, white coat all dirty. Sally said a mean thing about my curly tail. And my family changed my dog food to this awful blend of healthy bits that I can't stand."

Boris looked sadly at Prudence and thought, "What an attitude!" But what he said was, "Prudence, you sound really angry because life is not going your way today."

"Exactly! I took so much time today making myself pretty, and no one has even noticed or given me a compliment—and, what's worse, my hours of grooming were ruined by the mud all over my coat!" A big tear rolled down Prudence's pointed nose as she whimpered her tale of woe.

Boris was feeling quite annoyed because Prudence was being so negative, but he wanted to be supportive. He responded, "You feel disappointed because you were hoping for praise, but it's been the worst of days."

Prudence promptly broke down in sobs of sorrow and then resumed her pouting. While she was doing this, Boris decided that it wouldn't be helpful to Prudence to continue to console her. He realized that if he really wanted to help Prudence, as Prudence had helped him with his dancing, he would need to be more stern. He said, "Prudence, you're really having a pity party here. I'm wondering if you don't feel a little foolish seeing yourself as such a victim when you have so many privileges."

Prudence quickly stopped pouting and gave Boris a hurt and haughty stare. Full of pride, she retorted, "How dare you call me a victim—you're just a mutt with no pedigree!"

Boris paused, looked Prudence firmly in the eyes, and said, "Prudence, we're not talking about my breeding, we are talking about your behavior. You came here looking for me—I didn't come looking for you. All you've done since you came here is whine, complain, and pout. You need to get a grip and focus on something positive instead of wallowing in all the negatives you can accumulate."

Prudence, knowing that she sometimes let her appearance take on too much importance, hung her head and reluctantly acknowledged that Boris had a point. Then, much to Boris's amazement and to her credit, she said,

"Thank you, Boris. I'm going home to start my own gratitude book and write my own poem."

A week later, Prudence paid another visit to Boris. She showed him her first entry in her gratitude book:

> Sometimes you think a friend
> Is someone who will pretend
> That all you do and say is right.
> It's a dog who will let you whine
> Will say everything is fine
> And will never put up a fight.
> I learned that a friend does more
> Than just allow you to bore
> The world with all your complaints.
> A friend is like the cat
> Who won't let you be a brat
> And insists on some restraints.
> I needed to get a shock
> And to stop and take stock
> Of all my many gifts.
> Now I think about my bath
> And my ability with math
> To get me out of my fits.

Boris felt grateful that the risk he had taken by confronting Prudence with her bratty behavior had actually had an impact on her. After all, he had always liked Prudence and had appreciated her many talents, even though her prissy prancing sometimes made him mad. He got out his gratitude book and made another entry.

GUIDE FOR CHAPTER 16:

▼

BORIS LEARNS HOW TO LEARN

In this story, Boris takes charge of his own learning by resisting cultural distractions and meaningless expectations.

In preparation for this conversation, ask yourself what gets in the way of your learning—whether that learning is in the form of a course in continuing education or learning more about a family conflict or understanding your child's feelings.

This story deals with many of the issues that make learning difficult in our society. It also challenges children to go beyond rote memorization and superficial analysis. They can do this by:

➢ Making deeper connections

➢ Getting to the root causes of problems

➢ Overcoming one's history and bad habits

➢ Learning how to learn

➢ Inquiring without irritating

This story also conveys a simple, but powerful, learning methodology: explore, understand, and act. Exploration requires tolerance for ambiguity and a willingness to inquire deeply. Understanding requires rigorous analysis of options and objectives, which results in a concrete goal. Action requires disciplined implementation of a plan and diligent vigilance of progress. All of these elements of effective learning can meet with resistance in our culture.

In my experience, I have encountered many cultural obstacles to learning. In American society, many people prefer easy answers and are more focused on facts and concepts than they are on principles, skills, and objectives. However, what gives people the most satisfaction (the quick answer) does not necessarily give them the tools and insights they need to grow. I have found that learners are very pleased with programs that don't make them work too hard or confront their deficits.

As a result of responding to this story, you might find yourself engaged with the child in any or all of these questions:

- What obstacles might get in the way of your learning?

- Have you ever had a time when asking lots of questions has helped you to better understand a concept or topic?

- Which phase of learning do you prefer—exploration or action?

CHAPTER 16

▼

BORIS LEARNS HOW TO LEARN

Boris was tired of listening to the news on the TV in his doghouse. It was depressing to hear all the mindless talking about unimportant events in the world. After all, why would Boris care about a celebrity cat or a diva dog? The reporting seemed so shallow, and the topics they chose each night seemed absurd. The biggest news was about who got divorced and how much weight some dog had gained. Weren't there more important things to talk about?

Boris wondered how he could escape the negative influence of all the shallow news. He decided that he would pick the topics that interested him and learn as much as possible about them in order to get at the root of the causes and to make deeper connections. For example, he wanted to learn how the mind works and why people were so certain about their beliefs. He wanted to understand more deeply why violence was so prevalent in the world and what seemed to work best to bring about peace and harmony. Boris was determined to take charge of his learning. After all, he was almost five years old now.

Before heading off to the library to start his research, Boris trotted out to the pond to see his friend Zelda. He wanted to find out if Zelda felt the same way he did about the best ways to learn and how she was approaching her own learning and development.

After Zelda listened to Boris, she responded, "Boris, it sounds like you are tired of all the smug walking and smooth talking you see in the world. It makes you sick when you see dogs who are more interested in posing for the camera than making a difference in the world."

Boris looked at Zelda with amazement. Like always, she had been able to summarize what he had said in a way that not only affirmed his thoughts and feelings, but also gave him a fresh perspective on his problem. While she didn't use the same words Boris had used, she was able to summarize what he had said in a way that gave him something to think about and build on. He asked Zelda, "What can I do to improve the way I learn instead of just listening to what people on TV tell me?"

Zelda thought for a moment and replied, "Remember, sometimes you have to go through a period of confusion before you really understand something. I think there are three things you can do to learn about what's important to you. First, you need to be open to exploring many sources of information and not get anxious when you feel overwhelmed and confused. Second, you need to make sure that you are asking enough questions and using trusted sources so you don't jump too quickly to conclusions. Inquiry is the antidote to ignorance. That means that the best way to find out about something is to ask questions. Third, you need to learn from your actions. There is very little learning without action."

Boris felt his tail start wagging. He was very excited. It was the first time anyone had been able to teach him how to learn. His eyes got very big, and he started barking with joy. After he had calmed down a bit, Boris said to Zelda, "What you said sounds so simple. First, I need to explore the subject I want to learn about, and then I'll really understand it. After that, I'll act on what I've learned and then decide how well that worked. Everything seems so hard in school. I have to memorize, recite, and then I am tested. But now I can take charge of my own learning."

Boris left Zelda, feeling eager to try out his new learning skills. The first action he took was to turn off the TV and keep it off. He had had enough of reacting to what he heard instead of finding things out on his own. Second, he went to the library and looked for all kinds of different books on dancing. Boris had danced all his life, and he still loved to do it.

Finally, Boris started asking more questions. He was surprised to find that not everyone was pleased about his newly developed curiosity. They found his questions a little annoying because they had to take time from what they were doing to help Boris explore issues in which they were not particularly interested. For instance, when Boris asked Mr. Hamm, "Why should I learn how to act like normal dogs act?" Mr. Hamm's response was, "Because I told you so!"

Boris slumped off to his doghouse and asked himself, "Where can I find a group of dogs who enjoy learning as much as I do? I wonder what my brothers and sisters are learning these days." Boris knew that finding an answer to this question might take him some time, and he worried that he would never reconnect with his siblings. At least now he felt less depressed by the news on the TV, because he knew he had a choice to take other action and learn in a more active way.

GUIDE FOR CHAPTER 17:

▼

BORIS CONSIDERS HIMSELF IN THE MIRROR

In this story, Boris becomes Boris. He realizes how hard it is to develop a crystallized "I," that is, to discover the essence of who he is.

In preparation for this conversation, think about how you view yourself and how that "self" changes based on certain circumstances. Review a typical day. You wake up feeling a certain way, and then something happens to change your mood. For example, you may wake up feeling cheerful and positive and then get stuck in a traffic jam on the way to work. All of a sudden, you are grumpy, impatient, and irritable. You may arrive at work, and someone comments on how great you look. Suddenly, your spirit lifts, and you are feeling terrific again. Then the boss comes in and gives you negative feedback on a report you just wrote. Bam—you're in the dumps again. Ask yourself, how does "who I am" change in response to different conditions or expectations?

This story deals with just one big theme:

- unifying one's being

It deals with the challenges of being who we are under changing circumstances. Clearly, different conditions require different responses, but in the process of doing what we need to do and reacting to a given stimulus, do we lose track of our core being?

In my experience, a good rule is never to say "I" and think it is "you." That is to say, do not identify yourself as always being a certain way in all situations. Most of us tend to be fragmented. We seem to be different people in different situations. Sometimes our emotions take over and drive our behavior. Sometimes our bodies break down and we engage in behaviors that we typically abhor. Many times, we get so caught up in the culture that we lose track of becoming who we want to be.

An excellent example in the American culture is the celebrity craze people are often confronted with day after day. Athletes and actors are more dominant role models than scientists and scholars. In this culture, there is more emphasis on "doing" than on "being." College graduates are rarely asked, "Who are you going to be?" Instead, they are asked, "What are you going to do?"

As a result of responding to this story, you might find yourself engaged with the child in any or all of these questions:

- Who are you? How would you describe yourself?

- How do you react to changes in your daily routine?

- What is the most dominant dimension of your life: physical, emotional, intellectual, or spiritual?

- In what area of your life do you have the most interest: physical (for example, sports), emotional (for example, friendships), intellectual (for example, reading), or spiritual (for example, just sitting and reflecting)?

CHAPTER 17

▼

BORIS CONSIDERS HIMSELF IN THE MIRROR

Boris had just celebrated his fifth anniversary with the Hamms, and he was confused. It seemed like every day he would get up in a certain mood, and before he knew it, the mood had changed. Boris wondered why that was.

He thought, "Why can't I just wake up happy and stay that way all day long?" And yet Boris knew, in his infinite dog wisdom, that he couldn't be happy all day, every day. Sometimes, sad things happened in life. Other times, things happened to Boris that were scary—like the time a big dog from one of the scary gangs jumped up and growled at him. Still, it seemed to Boris that every time he looked in his mirror, he saw a different dog. He decided to keep his mirror in the bag he carried with him (Boris's version of a briefcase) for one full day and to look in the mirror at least once an hour. Maybe then he could solve the puzzle of who he was.

When Boris woke the next morning, he found his mirror and studied what he saw. To his great joy, he saw himself looking right back at him—a happy-looking, five-year-old, brown mutt who looked a little like a poodle, a little like a lab, and a little bit like many other types of dogs. Yes, the face in the mirror looked a lot like Boris expected it would.

He hopped out of his bed and trotted over to his purple dish expecting to find a full bowl of his favorite, delicious chow. Much to his surprise, he found the dish was half empty. When he glanced around wondering how this tragedy had happened, he saw that the screen door nearby was slightly open. Then he saw Phoebe, a neighborhood purebred, slinking away with a guilty look on her face. Boris barked at Phoebe and chased her away through the front yard. He was very angry.

His good friend, Zelda, who happened to be sitting quietly under a tree observing this whole scene, shook her big, hairy head and said to Boris, "I can't believe what I just saw. You looked more like a mean, ornery rascal than the sweet dog I know you to be. You have every right to be angry, but I'm surprised you let that dog push your buttons. You should take a look in that silly mirror you're always carrying around with you."

As he returned slowly to his dish, Boris decided to take Zelda's advice. What he saw confirmed his fear. Looking back at him in the mirror was a frowning and pouting pit bull. Boris almost fell over with the realization that he could look and act like such a different dog in the matter of moment. How could the mirror reflect this foul pit bull when he had expected to see a friendly, happy Boris? Boris could not believe his eyes, and he quickly stuffed the mirror back in his bag.

Boris was so shaken up that he couldn't even finish what remained of the food in his bowl. He decided to go outside and chase some squirrels. Boris loved to chase squirrels because they knew exactly how close they could let Boris get to them and still be able to get away. What he loved most was when the squirrels would race up a tree just out of his reach and then scold Boris for chasing them. Sometimes they even threw acorns down on him!

After playing this fun game for a couple of hours, Boris decided to look at his mirror again to see if that pit bull would still stare back at him. To his great surprise, instead he saw a beaming Burmese—a big, playful mountain dog with a smile on his face. Boris shook his head to see if he might be dreaming. His ears flopped happily all over the place. Boris quickly put away his mirror, wondering if he might be going a little crazy.

Boris decided he'd better go lie down and collect his thoughts. As he was settling into his nap, Sally Siamese saw her opportunity to give him a hard time. Just as Boris loved to chase the squirrels, Sally loved to pester Boris. She knew she could tease him and make him mad, but she also knew that at heart, Boris had a gentle spirit, so he would never hurt her.

Sally figured she had a good thing going. She could entertain herself by bugging Boris, but she wasn't worried that he would paste her a good one with his big, furry paw. What she didn't know was that Boris was not in the mood to be teased today. He was still a bit rattled because Phoebe had stolen his food and his mirror seemed to be telling him things that he didn't like to see in himself. So when Sally snuck up on Boris and jumped on his back, Boris did not respond in his characteristic carefree manner. He stood up quickly and whirled around in circles until Sally let go. He gave Sally a mean look, and he even growled at her and started toward her in a menacing manner.

When Sally felt herself backed in a corner by this unexpected behavior, she reached out and slapped Boris in the nose with her claw. She didn't mean to hurt her friend, but she had to send him a message that she was feeling threatened. Poor Boris was so startled that Sally would strike him that he let out a yelp and retreated to his rug in the corner.

As Boris was trying to shake off this latest humiliation, his mirror fell out of his doggie bag and reflected still another doggie image. This time Boris found himself looking at a terrified terrier. How embarrassing! He just could not figure out what was happening to him. He had begun the day feeling like he was on top of the world, but now he felt like the world was on top of him. He seemed to change from one moment to the next. What was most confusing to Boris was that *he* didn't even seem to be the cause of the changes—it was the things that went on around him that changed him.

Fortunately for Boris, when he returned to the kitchen, he found his bowl filled to the brim with his favorite dog chow. He gobbled it up and smiled in contentment. Boris quietly snuck over to his favorite sleeping spot, the couch in the living room, and snuggled up for a nice nap. Just before he started sawing off dog snores, he took one last glance in his mirror. Much to his relief, there was the Boris he knew staring right back at him with a contented smile on his mug. Boris fell asleep, still confused, but determined to get to the bottom of his many moods. He decided it was going to take him a long time to figure out how different dogs kept appearing in his mirror.

Guide for Chapter 18:

▼

Boris Meditates

In this story, Boris learns how to relax. He discovers that he needs to find a time and place where he can be by himself and practice a relaxation exercise.

In preparation for this conversation, reflect on your primary stressors. What causes you to get tense and irritable? How frequently do these stressors occur?

This story addresses the challenge of staying relaxed in a hectic and demanding world. There are three key themes in this story:

➢ Creating your own space

➢ Finding time for yourself

➢ Practicing relaxation

In my experience, I have found that different strategies for relaxation work for different people. Some people like to go for a run at the beginning or at the end of the day. Other people like to go out for a drink with their friends after work. Those who are more introverted are inclined to curl up in a comfortable chair and read a great book. Others find a time and place to pray or meditate. But one of the most basic, but powerful, tools for relaxation is to simply breathe deeply and observe the pattern and depth of your breathing.

As a result of responding to this story, you might find yourself engaged with the child in any or all of these questions:

- Where do you go to "get away from it all?"

- When do you find time to just be by yourself?

- How do you manage your stress? What works the best for you?

CHAPTER 18

▼

BORIS MEDITATES

Boris felt hyper and stressed out. He felt like he was constantly busy, with no time to just chill. If he wasn't playing fetch with Aidan and Liam, he was going for a walk with Mrs. Hamm or watching a movie with Mr. Hamm. Boris felt grateful that everyone wanted to include him in their plans, but it seemed like he never had a chance to just sit and do nothing.

In the middle of this thought, Lucky barked out, "Let's go chase squirrels, Boris."

So Boris romped off with Lucky to chase some squirrels. Just as he returned and stretched out on the porch, exhausted from sprinting from one tree to another, always just missing the squirrel as it would scamper up the tree, Prudence dropped by and wanted to chat.

Boris wanted to say, "Leave me alone, Prudence. I'm about to take a nap," but he just wasn't the kind of dog that could be rude. He believed that if someone needed attention, he had an obligation to provide it. Yes, Boris was a decent dog, though maybe a little too accommodating for his own good. So Boris perked up his ears and let Prudence know that he was interested in her story.

Once Prudence had finally trotted off the porch feeling good because Boris had listened so carefully to what she was saying, Boris sighed, smiled, and closed his eyes in peaceful reverie. Just as he was drifting off into his favorite dream of eating doggie biscuits on the beach, Gabby pounced on him and wanted to play catch me if you can. Once again, Boris dragged himself out of his blissful slumber and chased his friend around the house until both had had enough.

After that, Boris knew he needed to stop trying to be busy all the time and start just sitting for a while. Boris managed to sneak off into the woods to his favorite spot beside the pond where no one would bother him. Soon he was resting beside the pond, looking at the birds. He closed his eyes, took a couple of deep breaths, and thought about nothing but how the air came into and out of his nose as he relaxed and breathed.

As Boris concentrated on his breathing, he noticed how all of his muscles seemed to be getting longer and longer. He no longer felt tight and tense. Boris was amused that distractions kept popping into his head, but he simply pushed them out of his mind.

After a few minutes, Boris felt calm and still. His mind was clear. He felt at peace. He let more time pass. After about an hour of just being with himself and nature, Boris felt refreshed. He slowly got up, stretched, and began a slow walk back home.

Boris strolled out of the woods and went back to his porch. For some reason, the world looked different to him than it had when he was caught up in all the activity earlier. He noticed a hummingbird finding food in a flower. He heard a frog calling out, "Ribbit, ribbit."

When Lucky came over to play, Boris realized that Lucky seemed to calm down a bit, as well. Boris thought to himself, "I'm having more of an impact by doing nothing. By being calm, I'm having a calming influence on hyper Lucky." He concluded that maybe he didn't need to be so stressed out all the time. Sometimes, you just need to slow down.

Guide for Chapter 19:

▼

Boris Sizes Up His Friends

In this story, Boris assesses the strengths and weaknesses of his friends as well as their knowledge of their own strengths and weaknesses.

In preparation for this conversation, reflect upon your strengths and weaknesses.

This story addresses three key themes:

➢ Dealing with differences

➢ Owning your strengths

➢ Confronting your deficits

The story is about making an accurate assessment of one's assets and liabilities and understanding how to relate to people with different-looking "balance sheets."

In my experience, all three of these themes have presented challenges. As I was growing up, I liked everyone to be the same. I associated almost exclusively with bright white guys who loved sports, meaning I essentially avoided dealing with people who were very different from me. Also, while I probably went overboard in terms of owning my strengths (some would say I was cocky and arrogant), I resented any comments about my deficits.

While hubris and arrogance are not desirable traits, in some cultures, self-effacement goes too far. It's important to know what your strengths are and to be unapologetic about using them to make things better for yourself and for society. On the other hand, it is equally important to confront your weaknesses and to manage them. Many people put far more energy into eliminating deficits than leveraging strengths. It makes much more sense to invest in your strengths and simply manage your deficits. At the same time, it is critical not to engage in self-deception by denying your weaknesses, covering them up, or not even being aware of what they are.

As a result of responding to this story, you might find yourself engaged with the child in any or all of these questions:

- What are your biggest strengths? How do you make the most of them?

- What are your biggest weaknesses? How do you manage them?

- Do you have any friends who have no idea about their strengths and weaknesses? What are those traits?

- How difficult is it for you to say, "I'm really good at …?"

CHAPTER 19

▼

BORIS SIZES UP HIS FRIENDS

As Boris thought about his friends, he realized how different they all were. He had known them for almost six years now. On one level, it was irritating that he had to treat each one differently—that took a lot of work. On another level, Boris was fascinated and intrigued by the fact that all dogs had styles of their own and that all dogs saw themselves so differently. As he was sunning himself in the front yard, Boris thought about each of his best friends and how they were different.

Lucky seemed to know what he was good at, but he didn't seem to be aware of what he wasn't so good at. Lucky was terrific at barking at strangers, but lots of other dogs (and people, too) got pretty annoyed with all the noise he made. He knew that his family, the Knowleses, valued his protective instincts, but he didn't have a clue that all his barking caused many dogs to want to wear earplugs all day. Instead he just figured the other dogs admired his bravado and wished they could be more like him. Boris knew that Zelda would call that "delusional," which Boris understood to mean that Lucky had no idea how his behavior affected others.

Prudence, on the other hand, seemed very aware of her weaknesses, but didn't seem to have a good sense of her strengths. Prudence was always pouting about being smaller than the other dogs and not being able to catch a ball when someone would throw it. She would try her best to leap in the air and grab the ball in her teeth before another dog jumped five feet in the air—above her reach—and snatched it cleanly. Every time Prudence played this game, it ended the same way. She would slink off to her house, tell herself what a loser she was, and become very depressed.

The truth was that Prudence happened to be extremely talented in other areas of her life. She was very quick to learn new tricks. She was able to get along very well with all kinds of people and dogs; for instance, she entertained little children better than any other dog in the neighborhood. And of course she was a terrific teacher of dog dancing. Unfortunately, none of those strengths seemed to matter to Prudence. She wasn't aware of how many talents she had. All that she could focus on was her inability to catch a ball. In that regard, Prudence seemed to be stuck feeling bad about herself.

As Boris thought about which of his friends seemed to have a clear idea of what they did well and what they weren't able to do so well, Zelda popped into his mind. Zelda seemed to be very clear about her strengths, and she wasn't reluctant to say what they were. She knew she was very good at listening, solving problems, coming up with new ideas, and being able to impress even some very smart dogs. She was also aware of many of her weaknesses and wasn't afraid to admit them. Zelda knew she could be impatient (especially with foolish dogs), and she knew she wasn't the fastest runner on the block. Her bark was weak—Boris could hardly hear it unless Zelda was standing right next to him—and she couldn't dance very well. But what Boris admired about Zelda was her ability to make the most of her strengths and to manage her weaknesses. She didn't seem overly proud of her strengths or overly concerned about her limitations. She just did the best she could with what she had.

For some reason, thinking about Zelda made Boris think about the dog in his neighborhood who was the most unlike her. Paul Pitt didn't seem to have any idea what he did well *or* what he didn't do so well. In fact, he had the two totally turned around. Paul thought he was really good at making friends when, in reality, most dogs couldn't stand to be around him. He also viewed himself as a real pushover when, in truth, he always stood up for himself when he needed to. The sad thing about Paul was that he was entirely out of touch with who he was and who he had the potential to be if he used his strengths to their fullest.

By the time Boris had sized up all of his friends, the sun had risen high. His nose was hot and his mouth was dry. Boris decided to run in the sprinkler and get a nice, cool drink. "Lucky for me," Boris thought, "I've got my head on straight." Boris knew how important it was to know one's strengths and weaknesses.

GUIDE FOR CHAPTER 20:

▼

BORIS BELIEVES HE CAN FLY

In this story, Boris opens his mind and tests his beliefs against the evidence.

In preparation for this conversation, reflect upon your core beliefs.

This story highlights the negative themes that cause so much harm to the world at large as well in terms of personal growth and development. These are the three major negative themes:

➤ Holding onto beliefs independent of evidence that contradicts them

➤ Imposing one's beliefs on others

➤ Closing your mind to other possibilities

In my experience, passionately held religious and political beliefs represent real dangers when people refuse to look at scientific or historical evidence that runs counter to those beliefs. Since our beliefs are the basis on which we draw conclusions and behave toward others, it is critical that these beliefs are grounded in reality. I have found that people who base their beliefs on a limited depth and breadth of information sources tend to take the most extreme positions and tend to be closed to exploring different options or behaviors.

My belief, therefore, is that we need to challenge our beliefs by looking at multiple sources of information and by digging deep for whatever truth we can find. I also believe that individuals need to understand how their belief systems drive their behavior and lead to the conclusions they make. To me, doubt results in much better conclusions than certainty. It is important to stay open-minded and not close ourselves to the possibility that we could be wrong.

As a result of responding to this story, you might find yourself engaged with the child in any or all of these questions:

- What is one of your strongest beliefs?

- Has someone ever tried to tell you what you should believe? How did you react?

- Do you think your beliefs might change someday?

- Would your behavior change if one of your beliefs changed? In what ways? Why or why not?

CHAPTER 20

▼

BORIS BELIEVES HE CAN FLY

Boris believed he could fly. Oh yes, he truly believed this. He believed that dogs could fly as high as they wanted. Life held no limits for Boris, and he held onto this belief as tightly as he could.

Boris became so caught up in this belief that he started irritating his friends in the neighborhood by hounding them to share his belief. Whenever he tried to convince his canine friends about how dogs could fly, he would become very animated. His eyes would grow wide, his tail would wag furiously, his whole body would shake, and his bark would become shrill and loud. And when he heard about dogs in the next town who were trying to convince their friends that dogs could walk on stilts, Boris became furious. That belief conflicted somewhat with his belief (why would a dog need stilts if he could fly?), and he didn't like the idea of dogs preaching to others. It made him so mad that he wanted to go pounce on them. Boris, convinced that he was right in his belief, decided to form a club for all dogs who believed they could fly.

"Lucky, please join my new club. I know if we work really hard and get crazy creative, we can learn how to fly."

"Boris, you're out of your mind!" Lucky replied. "Dogs can't fly, and they can't walk on stilts. Why do you need these crazy beliefs in order to live your life? I'm perfectly happy just spending time with the Knowleses and occasionally sitting in Mr. Knowles's lap," Lucky sighed.

"Bah, you're a loser lap dog," Boris whined as he went away.

Boris persisted to pester his pet friends. Paul Pitt growled when he saw Boris coming. He was tired of hearing about all this flying nonsense. But when Paul tried to bully Boris out of his beliefs, Boris rudely ran away.

"Boris, did you notice that you don't have wings? That might make flying a little difficult," Gabby teased. Boris simply couldn't see how that changed anything. Gabby said, "Well, you can believe whatever you want, but I just want to hang out with the other dogs."

One day Boris bumped into Zelda. He appreciated the fact that Zelda didn't get upset when Boris told her he would someday be able to fly. She said to him, "You must feel excited because flying would give you a whole new view of the world. It must give you a real sense of comfort to be so sure about this belief."

But Boris got frustrated with her because when he asked her to join his cause, she politely refused. What Boris couldn't understand was why this wise dog didn't want to join his club.

One afternoon, after being very supportive of Boris's right to believe whatever he wanted, Zelda asked him, "Where did you learn about this flying belief, and how did you come to the conclusion that you could fly?"

Boris had to stop and think. Hearing that question felt a little bit like when he ran over his electric fence line and got a shock. "I read about flying dogs in this book I found in the library," Boris admitted. He took the book out from his doggie briefcase, the bag on his back.

Zelda looked at the book carefully and said, "Boris, this is a science fiction book. It's based on fantasy instead of facts."

Since Boris loved adventure, and sometimes being a little different, he had taken this one piece of information about dogs' ability to fly as being absolute truth. "You might want to explore other ideas about how to make life more of an adventure," Zelda advised. "Open your mind to other possibilities for making life the blast you think it should be. You know, Boris, the mind is like a parachute: it only works when it is open."

That statement stopped Boris in his tracks. It made him close his eyes, quit wagging his tail, and stop shivering all over as he thought. He barked softly, "Hmm, I guess I *should* explore other possibilities. Maybe then I wouldn't cling so fiercely to this conclusion I've made."

Even though Boris was not quite ready to give up his belief that with enough spring in his legs and desire in his heart he might someday be able to fly, he did decide that he needed to consider more facts and be open to other conclusions. He vowed to consider other ways to make his life as exciting and meaningful as possible.

As Boris pranced home that evening—because we all know that Boris loves to prance—he thought not only about his conversation with Zelda, but also about how the conversation with Zelda was so much different than the conversations he'd had with Lucky, Paul, and Gabby. Zelda hadn't dismissed his ideas just because they were different and a bit hard to believe. And with

Zelda, Boris did not feel judged. She simply asked him to look at more facts and to be open to different conclusions than the ones he was making. With the other dogs, Boris had not felt like he'd even been heard, and he did not feel like they respected his right to believe what he wanted, even if that belief was a little beyond what one might expect from a normal dog's life.

Boris dropped his idea of forming a club with dogs who all believed the same thing. Instead, he decided to join a club that invited dogs with all kinds of different beliefs. In the new club, it didn't matter what you believed. This club was only interested in how you thought and where you were finding new and exciting ideas. Lucky, Gabby, and Paul all barked with joy as they joined the CRITS Club: the Community for Rational and Innovative Thinkers.

GUIDE FOR CHAPTER 21:

▼

BORIS LEARNS ABOUT LEADERSHIP

In this story, Boris learns how to make a difference through effective leadership.

In preparation for this conversation, think about a time when you assumed a leadership role. What did you do? What was the outcome?

This story addresses the difficulties of making a difference and the leadership requirements for success. It highlights four major themes regarding successful leaders:

➤ Assessing level of functioning (i.e., evaluating team members for their skills and levels of ability)

➤ Finding support for your ideas

➤ Identifying the right talent for a job

➤ Creating an environment that supports your goals

Boris finds that the people closest to him don't have the commitment or capabilities needed to advance his vision of creating a healthy community. He has to look outside his small circle of friends and find some of the best thinkers in a larger circle. He also realizes that a culture tends to resist change until a certain tipping point is reached, which gives the reluctant people a sort of permission to join. For example, in America's history, when more and more people joined the civil rights movement, it reached a point where civil disobedience became "acceptable."

In my experience, it is very difficult to make a difference alone. Being successful requires collaboration and interdependence. Taking a hard look at the motivation and skills of potential participants in the movement can be a sobering experience, but it is a necessary one. Then, it is critical to find champions and advocates for the change—people who will actually contribute to its success. With those people in place, the team can work together to carefully craft a culture that supports the change.

As a result of responding to this story, you might find yourself engaged with the child in any or all of these questions:

- What's the biggest idea you have ever had for making a difference in the world or in your own life?

- In the past, how have you found support for your ideas? What happened if you didn't have any support?

- Who did you ask to help you?

- How did you go about enacting change?

CHAPTER 21

▼

BORIS LEARNS ABOUT LEADERSHIP

Boris thought about the various packs of dogs in the different neighborhoods and shook his head. To him, all the dogs seemed to be interested in the wrong things and were heading in the wrong direction. They seemed more interested in looking good than being good. After almost seven years with the Hamms, Boris was still waiting to find some friends who wanted to grow as individuals.

He thought about his current friends. The only thing Prudence wanted to grow was her hair. Lucky was only interested in gourmet doggie biscuits and making his doghouse bigger and bigger.

Boris asked, "Where is the leadership?" He knew it would take real leadership to change the way things were going. For example, Dick Dogbreath, a mean old dog who had somehow acquired a lot of power in a neighboring town, was always sending puppies to war in neighborhoods where dogs believed differently than he did. Growth was not in his vocabulary.

Boris decided to ask his friends if they would like to join a club that would create a new vision of what was possible for dogs. The purpose of the club would be to support each other's healthy goals.

However, when Boris asked his friends who might be interested, most of them said things like:

I like the status quo.
Why would I want to grow?
Don't tell me what I need.

And don't bother to take the lead.
I'm doing the best I can.
Just leave me alone, Bo.
Today I'm going to play.
I will grow another day.

Discouraged after all this rejection, Boris went to visit Zelda. As always, Zelda listened to the problem Boris shared with her. She responded to his unhappiness that no one seemed to understand him by saying, "Leadership is getting people to *want* to do what they need to do for their own growth or for your growth. You have to find a few dogs who share your desire to grow and show the other dogs what life can be like if you try to be the best you can be."

Boris decided if he was going to make a difference in his neighborhood, he would have to grow as a leader. First, he set out to find the dogs who shared his vision of what might be possible. He started his search full of energy and enthusiasm, but it turned out to be much harder than he had expected. There were a lot of dogs like Prudence, Gabby, and Lucky who weren't destructive, yet who just wanted to sit in their yards and watch the world go by. He even found several dogs who would play along with him, but Boris was looking for dogs who could actually contribute to his project, or even help him lead it. There weren't many of that type of dog around.

After months of scratching around and making long trips to other neighborhoods, keeping a careful watch out for dangerous gangs of mean dogs, Boris was able to recruit two other dogs who shared his goals. Allie Einstein was an extremely bright dog who was always coming up with wild ideas. Peter, the Great Dane, was a very big dog who was not only very inquisitive, but also very bold. Even though he came from an aristocratic family, Peter related well to all the other dogs and said he only wanted to free dogs to think differently.

Boris knew he only needed a few strong dogs to be able to show how life could be better than most of the other dogs could possibly imagine. Boris, Allie, and Peter met often to talk about what they might do to improve the sorry state that so many dogs had fallen into. They all knew that many dogs were lazy and numb to what was going on around them, so they tried to think of ways to help these dogs grow. They even used fancy new technology to make it easy for dogs to learn—Allie Einstein had the idea of giving all dogs iPods loaded with lots of music about their possibilities and potential for growth.

Boris, Allie, and Peter were amazed at how quickly dogs signed up for this new club when they heard about the iPods and got excited about heightening their potential. It wasn't long before they had seven dogs in their club, then twenty one. By the end of the first year, Boris, Peter, and Allie had signed up the hundredth dog, and they started to see things change in their town. Prudence started thinking about more than her hair. Lucky started building doghouses for homeless dogs. Unfortunately, Dick Dogbreath didn't change his ways, and Boris worried that he probably never would. This was a problem that he and his group of leaders would really need to think about for the future.

GUIDE FOR CHAPTER 22:

▼

BORIS MAKES A SOUL

In this story, Boris resists the seductive power of celebrity and focuses on creating a soul.

In preparation for this conversation, reflect upon the distractions in your life that have led you away from a higher purpose. For example, you may have been committed to a certain cause in your youth, only to drift away from it as you were faced with the responsibilities of raising a family.

This story deals with the temptations that divert our attention from the primary possibility in life: the opportunity to develop a soul. There are three major themes highlighted in this story:

➢ Being careful about what you wish for

➢ Resisting the need for attention and self-indulgence

➢ Staying true to who you are

In my experience, it's a constant battle to focus on who you are and who you want to become in a culture that is filled with distractions. While there are many options for spiritual development, I find that the most challenging and fulfilling one is to be in this world but not be caught up in all these distractions. Many people who are interested in spiritual growth have gone to ashrams, monasteries, convents, or other places that are removed from the real world. The limiting factor in those choices is that you decrease your chances of making a real difference in the world by secluding yourself. I believe that the key to living in this world, but not being seduced or corrupted by it, is to find time for solitude and reflection. Temporarily removing yourself from the buzz and business of the world can help to center you and restore a sense of calm. I do not believe we are born with a soul; I think we are born with the opportunity to make a soul.

As a result of responding to this story, you might find yourself engaged with the child in any or all of these questions:

- Do you have any wishes that, if they came true, could cause more problems than they are worth?

- When does the need for attention turn into selfishness?

- How do you stay focused on becoming who you want to be? What are the major distractions to this that you face?

- What does it mean to develop a soul?

CHAPTER 22

▼

BORIS MAKES A SOUL

Boris dreamed of being famous. When he sat in the living room wagging his tail and watching TV with the Hamm family, Boris became the most excited whenever a celebrity appeared on the tube. Everyone screamed, yelled, clapped, and yes, sometimes even shed tears of overwhelming joy when the star walked on the stage. For his part, Boris would start twirling around in circles and yelping as loud as he could. Needless to say, the Hamms weren't particularly pleased with these outbursts—or these inclinations, for that matter. He wanted so badly to create the same kind of wild frenzy when *he* pranced down the street.

In truth, Boris wanted both to become famous, *and* he wanted to have a noble excuse for becoming famous. Luckily, he did have such an excuse. He secretly hoped that his brothers and sisters might see him on television one day and they would find a way to get together. "How wonderful a way to connect back up with my siblings," Boris dreamed.

Boris thought and thought about how he could become famous. He remembered seeing old movies of Lassie, that loyal collie who was always involved in the heroic rescue of a reckless child. Boris had also heard about the legends of Rin Tin Tin, a German shepherd, who always could be counted on in times of crisis to do something extraordinary.

But as Boris thought about the dogs that were famous these days, he became totally confused. It seemed like the most famous dogs nowadays had either accumulated a lot of money through some crazy invention or were glorified for their long ears or wagging tail—despite not seeming particularly bright—or got a lot of attention for acting badly after they had recorded one best-selling album. Boris also reflected on how *people* seemed to get famous and then considered whether he might try to do so in the same way.

But Boris eventually decided he really didn't care how he became famous; he just craved the wild crowds, the signature seekers, and all the attention that people with cameras and microphones seemed to give celebrities. He also wanted to find a way to get together with his brothers and sisters; it didn't matter what the driving motivation was.

Boris became desperate to fulfill this need. The same poem kept playing over and over in his mind:

> I want to be a name
> I need to have great fame
> I want to be in lights
> I need to reach great heights

Boris thought that the way he would make this repeating rhyme a reality was to become a singer. He had heard about this television show called *American Idol*. On it, young people from all over the country entered a singing competition that would make them instantly famous if they won. The show inspired Boris to enter the canine equivalent: the World Rival competition for the best singing dog. This competition focused on country singing, and Boris could belt out a mean, nasal whine. He felt really excited that he had found his path to fame.

In a highly agitated state, Boris anxiously went out looking for just the right music for the competition. As he was frantically running from one store to another, he happened to bump into Zelda. Zelda noticed how crazed Boris was acting and said, "Boris, you look really worked up. What's going on with you?"

Boris couldn't wait to tell Zelda his plans. With wide eyes and wagging tail, his body shaking with excitement, he let her know what he was up to and how he was searching for the song that would launch him to stardom.

Zelda calmly listened to the whole story. When Boris had finished, a bit exhausted from telling the story tale and from his continually wagging dog tail, Zelda asked some unsettling questions. "Boris," she said, "how do you think your life would change if your dreams came true? What would happen if you got what you wished for?"

Boris excitedly sputtered out his answer: "All the dogs would adore me, everyone would want to take my picture, I could buy a fancy doghouse, and everyone would clap and scream when they saw me!"

Zelda looked hard into Boris's eyes and asked, "And that would be better than the life you have now?"

Boris was a little shocked by the question. He had to admit that having too little privacy and too much praise might not help him become the dog he really wanted to be. Zelda breathed a little sigh of relief. She said, "I am really happy to hear you admit that this desire of yours might lead you away from who you want to be. I have always considered you a very thoughtful dog who enjoyed having time to think and to help others. I admire the ways in which you have created peace among the different dogs and the way you relate to children. I hope you will think about the dangers of getting what you wish for—at least in this case."

Boris slumped his shoulders, let his head drop, and slowly returned to his doghouse. He had been really excited about becoming famous, and he hated to let go of that dream. And, sadly for Boris, he really did have talent and actually had a chance of making his first poem a reality. He knew deep in his heart, though, that it was more important to make a soul for himself than to make a name for himself. Making a soul meant clearly defining who he was and knowing deep inside what was most important to him. So, though perhaps a little reluctantly, Boris made up a new poem that might lead him to who he really was and wanted to be:

> I want to make a soul
> Though I know it takes a toll
> I always need to reflect
> If I ever hope to perfect
> Who I am and who I can be.

Boris still wondered, though, how he was going to find his brothers and sisters. He wasn't ready to give up on that dream, which he felt was part of his journey to creating his soul.

GUIDE FOR CHAPTER 23:

▼

BORIS TRIES TO INSPIRE OTHERS

In this story, Boris learns that because most individuals in the world want so little, they often don't really work to try to give too much.

In preparation for this conversation, think about the times when you were really excited about an idea that very few people cared about. You were ready to give your all to a project, but you couldn't find any support for your effort.

This story deals with the reality that few people want to venture outside of traditional norms and conventions. History has demonstrated time and again that being at the extremes of the bell curve gets you punished, whether you are on the low end or on the high end. People who read these Boris stories are unlikely to have had the experience of being punished for falling on the low end of the curve. It is precisely the people who read these stories, however, who are likely to get punished for being on the high end of the curve. For example, Reich was thrown in jail for his ideas, Nietzsche was ridiculed, and Einstein was denied faculty jobs in physics.

The following story illustrates three lessons for unconventional outsiders who are trying to make a difference in the world:

➢ It's more about trying to be the best you can be than imposing your views on others.

➢ It's important to assess the level of functioning of the person with whom you are talking before offering a challenging point of view.

➢ Make sure you enter the frame of reference of others before you try to educate them.

In my experience, I have failed many times to inspire people to try a different approach. When I became too enthusiastic about my ideas, most listeners either tuned out or were turned off. I found I had the biggest impact when I first entered the other person's frame of reference, then continued to remember who I was talking to. I learned that if I simply tried to do the best I could, my behavior and the results I achieved had more impact than trying to convert people to my way of thinking.

As a result of responding to this story, you might find yourself engaged with the child in any or all of these questions:

• What has been your experience whenever you've tried to tell someone about an idea you had?

• Is there anyone you know who works really hard to be the best they can be?

• How have your friends reacted at times when you have tried to do your best?

• Have you ever tried to convince others to push their own limits?

• Do you know anyone who has been treated badly for trying something different—going against the crowd?

CHAPTER 23

▼

BORIS TRIES TO INSPIRE OTHERS

Boris continued to wonder how he could make a difference in his world. Despite all the work he had done toward becoming a community leader and trying to motivate others, he was still disturbed by the dogs that seemed content to just lie around and watch life pass them by. Boris believed that the purpose of life was to develop, so he decided to start a school that could help others with this goal. He called it the School of Possibilities.

Boris got so excited about this idea that he started cleaning up the Hamm's backyard, where he decided to hold classes. He figured he could climb up on top of his doghouse to lead these lessons. Boris beamed with enthusiasm at the thought of being a teacher of possibilities.

When Boris started inviting his friends to his new school, he was met with mixed reactions. Zelda thought it was a terrific idea and said she would be pleased to join. Prudence and Gabby seemed a bit hesitant, but they agreed to come to the first class to see what these "possibilities" were that Boris was talking about.

"I'll wait to hear what the others have to say after the first class," Lucky responded.

Paul simply growled, "There is no possibility of me attending any such nonsense school."

After three weeks of scouring the neighborhood for students in the new school, Boris managed to get twenty dogs to sign up for the first class. Now that the School of Possibilities had a decent-sized class, it suddenly seemed real. Boris, very pleased that his idea was coming to fruition, scrambled to prepare the first lesson.

After scratching his head with his paws and rolling in the dirt for several days, he finally came up with the idea of comparing life to a horse-drawn carriage. He would discuss how there are many kinds of carriages, many kinds of horses, many kinds of drivers, and many kinds of passengers. Boris thought endlessly about his opening talk. He hoped that his comments might get all of the dogs really excited about this School of Possibilities.

When opening day arrived and only ten dogs showed up, Boris was angry. He had to acknowledge his anger and let it go. After all, those twenty dogs had said they were going to show up. He felt his anger was justified, but he also knew there was nothing he could do. He would just have to make do with the students he had.

After he worked through his own emotions, here is what he said to the class: "Life is like a horse and carriage. Our emotions are characterized by the horse. Our body is the carriage. The cab driver symbolizes our minds. These components are loosely connected by the shaft between the carriage and the horse and the reins between the cab driver and the horse. Sometimes, the reins go free, and the carriage is pulled wildly by the horse, who has no idea where she is going. Other times, the carriage breaks down and needs repair. Occasionally, the driver gets sleepy and loses his way. Plus, over time, the carriage carries lots of different passengers. Some of the passengers are kind and loving, while others can be mean and nasty. The carriage attracts different passengers in different conditions. Storms attract one kind of passenger, and sunny days attract a different kind. These people all pass through the carriage and make little attempt to bring harmony among the carriage, the cabby, and the horse. Very rarely, the same passenger returns again and again to the carriage and tries not only to bring harmony, but also to become master of the three."

During the talk, Boris noticed that many of the dogs were fidgeting and playing with their tails. At the end, Boris looked around the yard from the top of his doghouse and found a wide range of reactions. Zelda, of course, was sitting up straight, leaning forward, and her eyes were bright with wonder. Prudence and Gabby were scratching their ears and barking at a cat that happened to be passing by. The rest of the dogs were sound asleep. When Boris asked his students how his story related to a dog's life, even Sally Siamese crossed her eyes.

Boris was disappointed and sad. After all, the story had made perfect sense to him. We need to tame our horses, keep our carriages in great repair, train a cab driver to drive down the right path and, hopefully, limit the passenger list to people we really admire. He decided that, in his next lesson, he would have to pick a smaller idea. He also learned that it would probably make sense to ask the dogs what they were hoping to learn in this new School of Possibilities. Boris was confident his next lesson would be a greater success.

GUIDE FOR CHAPTER 24:

▼

BORIS TEAMS UP WITH HIS FRIENDS

In this story, Boris learns the value of collaboration.

In preparation for this conversation, think about the times you were able to collaborate with others and create something that was better than what you would have been able to create on your own.

This story highlights some of the key ingredients of effective collaboration:

➤ Engaging others

➤ Sharing ideas

➤ Being open to others' ideas

➤ Building on others' ideas

➤ Empowering others to lead

In my experience, modern American culture reinforces fierce individualism. People are rewarded more for competing and acting independently than they are for working collaboratively and interdependently. It is not uncommon in organizations for people to make unilateral decisions without taking the time to engage others, seek out better ideas, and empower others to take risks. When there is a high level of collaboration, innovation improves, as well as the quality of products, services, and solutions.

As a result of responding to this story, you might find yourself engaged with the child in any or all of these questions:

- When have you had to collaborate on a project? How did it turn out? Do you think your team created a better product than you would have on your own?

- What has been your experience when people made decisions that affected you but didn't bother to ask for your thoughts and feelings before the decision was made?

- In what situations do you feel empowered to make your own decisions? How have your decisions turned out in those cases?

CHAPTER 24

▼

BORIS TEAMS UP WITH HIS FRIENDS

Boris knew he couldn't do everything he wanted to do on his own. He hated the idea of being dependent on the Hamm fam for food and housing, and he found himself competing with other dogs on things that didn't really matter, like who had the biggest doghouse, the prettiest fur, or the longest tail. Boris had always tried to be an independent thinker, but he realized that the projects he had started on his own weren't making the progress he had hoped for. He felt discouraged because more dogs had not joined his dancing dogs group, his School for Possibilities, his CRITS Club, or his helping kids read program.

Boris realized that maybe he wasn't doing enough to involve others in the projects he was thinking about. He rounded up Gabby, Lucky, and Prudence to talk about this.

"Not another club!" Lucky exclaimed when Boris invited him to this meeting of neighborhood dogs.

"Boris, I hope this isn't about another one of your crazy ideas," Gabby stated as she hesitantly sauntered down the road to the Hamm house.

"Oh, Boris, what grand scheme are you considering this time?" Prudence teasingly inquired.

Because they all loved Boris in spite of his quirky idiosyncrasies, they all showed up despite their doubts. After several years of living together, Boris's friends knew that he tended to get excited about wild ideas that had little chance of becoming real. They had come to understand, however, that occasionally some of his ideas were worth considering.

Once the group was gathered, Boris launched into his new idea with characteristic enthusiasm, but he was quickly interrupted. "Slow down, Boris. You're talking so fast I can't understand what you're saying," Lucky pleaded.

"You want to form a book group?" Prudence asked incredulously.

Gabby scratched her paws in the dirt and cocked her head. "Who would choose the books?" she asked, knowing Boris's history of wanting to make all the decisions and call all the shots.

Boris responded, "I know you're all a bit reluctant because not all of my ideas have resulted in much. And true, I may have made all the decisions on my own in the past, but I think this may be a good idea. We would rotate who picked the book each time we met."

Lucky, Gabby, and Prudence all looked at each other. Lucky noticed that Gabby was slowly shaking her head, and her ears were perked up. Prudence observed that Lucky wasn't rolling his eyes—a habit he had when he heard ideas he didn't like.

"Boris, it sounds like a good idea. Let's give it a shot," Gabby barked out enthusiastically.

Boris was thrilled that his friends supported the idea. He bolted to his doghouse and ran back to the group with a book in his mouth. "Here's the first book we could read!" he yelped out, his tail wagging furiously and his eyes open wide.

"Whoa, Boris!" his friends chided. "We thought we had a say in what books we would read and where we would discuss them."

"But … but … but …" Boris stammered. "I was just trying to be helpful and get us started."

"We know," Prudence said reassuringly. "It just would be nice for us to have a voice in the first decision."

Boris let the book drop from his mouth and apologized. "You're right. Let's talk about what a good first book might be."

Lucky suggested a book he had seen about dog sled racing. Gabby offered to look in the library for a book on famous dogs. Prudence wondered if they should start with a mystery story or a history of the town in which they lived.

Boris chimed in, "How about studying dogs in other parts of the world?"

After a long discussion, they decided on an autobiography of a dog who had hiked across the whole country. They were all excited about reading the book and discussing it.

"When should we meet?" Prudence asked. They agreed that three weeks would be a good amount of time for them to all read the book and think about it some.

"We can have our first meeting at my house," Lucky offered.

"I can bring some of my favorite snacks to share," Prudence volunteered.

Boris just smiled and supported the plan, knowing that sometimes a group is better than an individual.

GUIDE FOR CHAPTER 25:

▼

BORIS CATCHES HIMSELF STRETCHING THE TRUTH

In this story, Boris learns the importance of impartial objectivity.

In preparation for this conversation, ask yourself if you have ever been excited about something that you experienced and embellished the facts in the retelling of the story.

This story highlights the importance of holding ourselves to the truth. It deals with the ability to take a hard look at the facts even when they don't paint a compelling or exciting picture. There are two main themes in this story:

➢ Describing your experiences objectively

➢ Resisting hyperbole

In my experience, I have been known to get excited about an idea and, in the process, use superlative words that weren't necessarily appropriate or accurate. For me, maintaining objectivity is particularly difficult when I care about an idea or a person. Because I want to sell the idea or promote the person, I may inflate the truth or let partiality color my description.

It's especially hard to be impartially objective when we are evaluating our own behavior. We are vulnerable to self-deception because we would prefer to hold a favorable view of ourselves.

As a result of responding to this story, you might find yourself engaged with the child in any or all of these questions:

- Have you ever told a story in a way that bent the truth? How much did you exaggerate?

- Which of your friends, if any, tends to exaggerate details? Is it a habit of theirs, or just an occasional occurrence?

- How open are you to feedback on your own behavior? If you tend to stretch the truth or overexaggerate, are you willing to admit it if someone calls you on it?

CHAPTER 25

▼

BORIS CATCHES HIMSELF STRETCHING THE TRUTH

Boris had a bad habit of exaggerating the truth. He would get so excited when he told a story that sometimes the story just seemed to take over and lose all connection to reality.

"Hey, Lucky," Boris yelled out one morning. "You should have seen the butterfly I saw today. It was red, yellow, and black, and it was *huge*! It was bigger than that bird over there!"

Lucky rolled his eyes. "Boris, those are monarch butterflies. They are big and beautiful, but they are not as big as that bird."

"Well, the one I saw was that big," Boris said as he huffed down the street to see Gabby.

Boris liked to hang out with Gabby because she was always friendly and sometimes shared treats with him. Plus, she liked to hear Boris's stories. "Did you hear about the fish I caught in the pond yesterday?" Boris began, his tail wagging as he recalled the bluegill he caught and turned into this tall tale. "It was a monster fish! I think it may have been the biggest fish ever caught in any of the lakes around here."

"How big was it?" Gabby asked with a twinkle in her widening eyes.

Boris drew a sketch of the fish on the ground for Gabby to see. The drawing made it look like Boris had caught a whale instead of a bluegill.

Gabby cocked her head and looked at Boris skeptically. "That looks a little big for a bluegill, Boris. I know you're proud and excited, but that story is as hard to swallow as a fish that size would be."

Boris's tail stopped wagging. "Well, it was good to see you, Gabby," he mumbled as he trotted slowly down to Prudence's house.

"Hi, Boris. How are you today?" Prudence asked politely.

"*Great*!" Boris replied, though he didn't really feel that way at all after the way the others had reacted to his stories.

"How are you doing with your new dance routine?"

Boris's eyes brightened as he raised his chin. He could feel the excitement churning in his stomach as he prepared to tell Prudence all about his new moves. "I think I've come up with some jumps and turns that will guarantee a victory in this year's competition!" Boris barked out before he had thought about how that might sound to Prudence. Even as the words left his mouth, he started feeling foolish about having gotten carried away with Lucky and Gabby, and now having boasted to Prudence. "Maybe I should tone myself down a bit," he thought.

After a pause, Boris continued. "Well, they might not guarantee a victory. But I do feel good about these moves, and I've been working hard to perfect them."

Prudence smiled and said, "I'm glad you're still improving those steps, and I'll be there to support you when the competition takes place. Let me see how they look."

With that Boris broke into dance and strutted his stuff. He decided that instead of using big words, it was better to be modest and let the actions themselves do the talking.

GUIDE FOR CHAPTER 26:

▼

BORIS WAKES UP

In this story, Boris learns how to increase his consciousness.

In preparation for this conversation, reflect on those moments in your life when you were fully present and conscious—completely alert to what was unfolding in front of you. Being fully aware means that your whole being—physically, emotionally, intellectually, and spiritually—is completely "there" in the moment. What was your experience? Where were you? Did time seem to slow down? What did you notice that you wouldn't have noticed if you had been daydreaming, caught up in the flow of events, or simply not paying as much attention?

This story deals with the most fundamental requirements of spiritual development:

➢ Being fully present in the moment

➢ Paying close attention to surroundings and events

➢ Connecting deeply to other people

In my experience, there are only fleeting moments when I am fully focused and conscious. Since I have Tourette syndrome, I use the tics to remind me of how calm and still I am in any given moment. There is so much pull in our culture to get caught in the fast pace of life that it is difficult to just be still and observe yourself, your environment, your loved ones, or other people.

As a result of responding to this story, you might find yourself engaged with the child in any or all of these questions:

- At what times do you feel the most alert and alive?

- How does your experience differ when someone is fully paying attention to you versus when they seem distracted?

- What does it take to really connect with someone? How does the relationship change in those moments?

CHAPTER 26

▼

BORIS WAKES UP

"Boo!" Lucky barked.

Boris jumped up from the porch. He had been off in la-la land dreaming about his next great adventure. Lucky laughed at how easily he had been able to sneak up on Boris and scare him. "You're always somewhere else," Lucky teased as Boris tried to pull himself together.

"You caught me by surprise," Boris protested, trying to defend himself from Lucky's verbal jabs.

"It sure is easy to catch you by surprise," Lucky continued poking nonetheless. "You spend so much time dreaming about new schemes that you miss what's happening right in front of that long nose you have."

Boris knew that Lucky would continue to tease him unless he could change the subject. "What would you like to do today, Lucky? Swim in the lake? Walk back to the pond? Chase cats?"

Lucky stopped his teasing and asked, "What do you have in mind?

After debating all the options, Boris and Lucky decided to take a stroll to the pond in search of mushrooms, butterflies, and squirrels. And who knows—Zelda might even be hanging out back there. Lucky never really appreciated or understood Zelda, but he knew he could lie down and take a nap if she and Boris got into one of their endless conversations. Lucky was already imagining the spot he liked under the pine tree, which always had a nice breeze blowing off the pond.

"Boo!" Boris yelled at Lucky, teasing him about his mind being somewhere else. "You just missed a beautiful cardinal sweeping right past our heads." They laughed at how they were both guilty of missing what was going on in the moment because they were thinking about an event in the past or a possibility in the future.

As the two friends trotted down the trail, they found endless amusements to entertain themselves. First, a squirrel dropped an acorn on Lucky's head. They sprinted to the tree trying to scare the mischievous creature, but the squirrel just scolded them for being such pests. It seemed like squirrels were always getting the best of the dogs—in their rush to do battle, they had passed right by a whole field of their favorite mushrooms without even noticing.

Boris and Lucky crossed the bridge over the creek, and on the other side, Lucky spotted a hawk perched on a branch high up in a tree. The canines were a little nervous that the hawk might see them as his next meal, but being together bolstered their confidence. They watched the hawk for a few minutes, fascinated by its size and constant vigilance on the lookout for food. Finally, the hawk flew away, no doubt to look for a mouse or some other unsuspecting prey—hopefully not two hapless dogs not paying attention to the dangers lurking in the forest.

Zelda was deep in meditation when they arrived at the pond. Lucky thought it would be fun to sneak up on her and bark "Boo!" Boris was reluctant to play a trick on his friend and disturb her peace, but he crouched down behind Lucky, and they approached Zelda as slowly and quietly as they could. They avoided twigs and crunchy leaves and placed each paw softly on the ground as they inched toward their unsuspecting target.

Zelda looked up calmly. "What are you two bozos trying to do? I heard you coming a half mile away! You think you are so clever." She smiled and shook her head. "Hey, what are you guys up to today, anyway?"

Lucky's chin dropped down and his face got bright red. "I guess I'll go take a nap," he said. He slowly meandered toward his spot under the pine tree feeling embarrassed at his failed attempt to be sneaky. He slipped under the branches, found a comfortable spot on the ground, and fell quickly to sleep.

As Boris and Zelda walked quietly around the pond, Boris was amazed that his friend had been so aware of her surroundings. He asked his wise friend, "How did you know we were coming? You always seem very conscious of what's going on around you. The question is, how can I stop falling asleep all the time, even when I'm awake?"

GUIDE FOR CHAPTER 27:

▼

BORIS MOVES UP THE SCALE

In this story, Boris learns that his goals need to change as he grows older and wiser.

In preparation for this conversation, think about your goals. Which ones are physical? Emotional? Intellectual? Spiritual? How have you had to change them as you grew older?

This story addresses the need to:

➢ Set realistic goals

➢ Grow as others grow, or even if they don't.

In my experience as a coach, I have found that people get stuck in a certain level of development and resist making the effort to break through to the next level. This suggests that there are different levels of functioning that can be objectively evaluated. Many people don't like that idea.

At a very generic level, I believe there are seven levels of human development:

At level 1, people are physically dominant—fitness, money, and material concerns guide them.

At level 2, people are emotionally dominant—sentimental, religious, and social concerns rule.

At level 3, people are intellectually dominant—they are career-oriented, academic, and bookish.

At level 4, people are balanced. They are trying to grow multi-dimensionally.

At level 5, people are unified. They have a defined essence and no incongruent behaviors.

At level 6, people are conscious—fully awake and aware in all moments.

At level 7, people are perfected. They are capable of healing others and a powerful presence.

As a result of responding to this story, you might find yourself engaged with the child in any or all of these questions:

- What are your goals physically, emotionally, intellectually, and spiritually?

- How have you had to change your goals as you grew older and wiser?

- In what areas of your life are you out of balance?

CHAPTER 27

▼

BORIS MOVES UP THE SCALE

Boris struggled with setting goals. He had just celebrated his seventh anniversary with the Hamm fam, and he was trying to decide how he wanted to be seen by them as he grew older. After all, he was no longer a puppy, and he had even emerged as a promising leader of dogs in the neighborhood. Over the past few weeks, different members of the family had referred to him in a variety of ways and had treated him accordingly.

Aidan viewed Boris as a trustworthy friend. When he was feeling bored or lonely, Aidan would always seek out Boris and talk to him about his feelings. "Hey, Boris," he would say, "are you as bored as I am? Let's go outside and play catch."

Liam saw Boris as the best companion one could possibly have. "Can Boris come?" Liam would always ask, no matter where the Hamms were going.

"Oh, Boris is such a great dog!" Mrs. Hamm would laugh when her friends were visiting and Boris had to make sure he properly greeted everyone by sniffing their hands and wiggling all over.

Mr. Hamm seemed a little more reserved toward Boris. "Do you love Boris?" Aidan would ask his dad whenever he didn't think that Mr. Hamm was giving the dog enough attention.

Occasionally, Mr. Hamm was scolded by the family by referring to Boris as an irritating nuisance. Even though Mr. Hamm really did love Boris, he would sometimes come home from work feeling grouchy. Boris, noticing that Mr. Hamm was not in the best of moods, would snuggle up to him and put his head on his lap. But Mr. Hamm would shoo him away because he preferred to have some quiet time when he arrived home. Liam and Aidan had figured that out a long time ago. Boris was not only slower to learn, but more persistent in giving affection.

Boris was confused by this range of reactions to him. He wanted to be loved all the time by everyone. He was pondering about how he might achieve this goal as he wandered to the pond one afternoon.

"You look puzzled," Zelda said when she saw Boris approaching.

"I am totally confused," he replied. "I want to be loved by everyone all the time, and I can't figure out how I'm ever going to accomplish that."

Deep down inside, Boris still smarted from being abandoned as a puppy. When she asked what he meant by his comment, Boris proceeded to tell Zelda the different ways he was treated by each member of the Hamm family.

As ever, Zelda had sound advice for her friend. "For starters, Boris, I think your goal may be a little unrealistic. It's impossible to be loved by everyone all the time. Based on what you said, you might think about using a scale I came up with—a way to define different levels, to assess where you are and where you want to be."

Zelda described her scale to Boris as he paid close attention:

5:    Trusted member of the family
4:    A valued companion
3:    A great dog
2:    A fun pet
1:    An irritating nuisance

"I want to be a trusted member of the family!" Boris barked enthusiastically, his tail wagging fast. "But I'm not sure how I would do that …" His tail slowed to a much less rapid rate as he thought about his conundrum.

"To begin with," Zelda responded, "you will need to continue being a fun pet, a great dog, and a valued companion. You should also be sure you're never being an irritating nuisance. Think about what else you would need to do to become a trusted member of the family. You may need to have a different goal for each member of the family. You have to decide what level you want to have with each person and then move up the scale. With Aidan, it sounds like you are already a trusted member. But as he grows, you will need to grow, as well."

Boris nodded his head. "Thanks, Zelda," he said with a far-off look in his eyes and a frowning face. "I guess I'll head back home and give that some more thought." Boris knew that with time, he could be seen as a valued member of the family, even by a sometimes grumpy Mr. Hamm.

GUIDE FOR CHAPTER 28:

▼

BORIS GETS IT TOGETHER

In this story, Boris learns how to clarify his values and set priorities.

In preparation for this conversation, write down your most important values. What are your most important physical, emotional, intellectual, and spiritual values and goals?

This story addresses the spiritual challenge of feeling fragmented. It suggests that there are three areas of focus that could help one get it all together:

➤ Clarifying your values

➤ Prioritizing your time usage to meet your goals

➤ Engaging life in all dimensions: physically, emotionally, intellectually, and spiritually.

In my experience, being free means having no choice. What I mean is, as your values become clearer and clearer, you are less and less conflicted about what to do or how to spend your time. I have found that as my values come into clearer focus, it is easier for me to set priorities and make good use of my time. Since we have a limited amount of time on earth, it's vital to define what's most important to us so that we can use our time to satisfy our values.

As a result of responding to this story, you might find yourself engaged with the child in any or all of these questions:

- What are your values? What's most important to you?

- How well do you feel you use your time?

- How consistent are your behaviors with your values?

- Who are the people in your life who have the widest range of interests?

CHAPTER 28

▼

BORIS GETS IT TOGETHER

Boris was torn. He felt like he was being pulled in many directions. Forces both outside and inside himself seemed to shape the way he felt, the way he thought, and the way he viewed his role in the world.

Whenever Boris saw Gabby, he wanted to share his feelings. Whenever he played with Prudence, he wanted to talk about his latest dance step. Whenever he saw Lucky, he wanted to talk about his new technique for chasing squirrels. Whenever he saw Zelda, he wanted to discuss his current life struggles.

"Hey, Boris!" Lucky called out. "How did you like that story about the duck who couldn't swim?"

"Hey, Boris!" Gabby jumped in. "You sure looked angry when that squirrel dropped an acorn on your head!"

"Hey, Boris! Prudence chimed in. "How's that spin move coming? Doing that move while standing on your head must be quite a challenge. It's pretty funny to see your feet flailing and your ears flopping while you are spinning on your head at ninety miles an hour."

"Boris," Zelda inquired, "is that new club turning out to be everything you hoped it would be?"

Boris turned from one friend to another. He felt like his head was spinning, and he wasn't even doing his latest dance move. "Hold on!" Boris gasped. "Let's take one thing at a time."

Hanging out with his friends wasn't the only time Boris felt pulled apart. "Boris, you should exercise today," his conscience called. "Boris, you just need to relax," another voice butted in. "You really need to finish that book you were reading," something whispered in his ear. "You should visit your friends today," still another voice nagged at him. And deep inside, he still yearned for a way to find his brothers and sisters.

Boris lay down on his back with his feet lying limp on his body. His tail was stretched out behind him flat on the ground. He just shook his head. "There's too much going on both outside me and inside me," he thought to himself. "I love my friends, but they all have different ideas about how I should spend my time. And those voices in my head are driving me nuts! Even my internal voices seem to be at war with each other. They all have different ideas about how I should live my life."

Boris rolled back onto his belly and struggled to his feet. His fur was covered with leaves from rolling on the ground. As he headed to the pond to think everything through, he said to himself, "I need to get it together."

"Boris, you looked a bit disoriented earlier today," Zelda said as she approached the pond later in the afternoon.

"I just can't deal with all these options," he replied, still feeling dazed and confused.

"You can't decide whether to be a physical Boris, an intellectual Boris, an emotional Boris, or a spiritual Boris," Zelda suggested.

"I have so many interests, and I don't know which to pursue!" he said, his ears drooping.

"You don't have to choose," Zelda counseled. "The goal is to have balance in your life and to get all your parts lined up and working together."

Boris brightened. It seemed like such a reasonable suggestion. "I'll have to think about that one," he replied, standing straighter with his ears perked toward the sky.

"If you were clear about what was *most* important to you, these choices wouldn't cause you such angst," Zelda continued. "As your values become clearer, so do your priorities."

"What's angst?" Boris asked.

"Angst is simply a feeling of dread or anxiety arising from an awareness of free choice," Zelda answered.

"Hmmm, now I understand that saying I've heard before: freedom means having no choice." Boris scratched his chin with his big paw and trotted off with a bounce in his step. With these words of advice in his head, even the path back home seemed clearer.

GUIDE FOR CHAPTER 29:

▼

BORIS TAKES A RISK

In this story, Boris learns the difference between risk taking and thrill seeking.

In preparation for this conversation, reflect on a time when you were trying to learn a new skill or do something entirely outside your comfort zone.

This story addresses the requirements for skill mastery and the role of support in that process. There are three key themes:

➤ Practicing makes perfect

➤ Pushing may be necessary, but it should take into account the skill level of the person

➤ Seeking thrills involves assessing risks

In my experience, high levels of proficiency in any area can only be achieved through disciplined practice and hard work. The literature on success suggests that people at the top of their field put in at least ten thousand hours of practice over the course of their lives, whether that means playing a musical instrument, excelling in theoretical physics, or playing hockey. My ten thousand hours as a counseling psychologist were logged by facilitating meetings with inmates, psychologists, teachers, counselors, nurses, and business executives.

As a result of responding to this story, you might find yourself engaged with the child in any or all of these questions:

- What gives you the greatest thrill? Were there skills required to experience that thrill? How do you prepare yourself for the experience?

- Do you feel that you are proficient in any area—a subject of knowledge or sport, for example? How hard and long did you have to practice to achieve that level of proficiency?

- Have you ever sought a thrill without assessing the risks? What was the result?

- Has anyone ever pushed you to achieve greatness? How did you react to the pressure? Did you get better as a result?

CHAPTER 29

▼

BORIS TAKES A RISK

"Come on, Boris, this road is smooth and flat. It's a perfect spot to practice," Lucky encouraged with a twinkle in his eyes.

Boris put his front two paws on the skateboard and gave a strong push with his back legs. Whoosh! The board went flying, and so did Boris as he tumbled over. "Yikes!" Boris hollered. "This isn't as easy as it looks."

"Aw, you'll get the hang of it after a few tries," Lucky said, urging on his friend.

After many more failed starts, Boris finally was able to stay balanced on the board for a nice, smooth ride.

"Great job!" Lucky barked enthusiastically. "Now let's try a small hill."

Boris gulped twice, grabbed the board in his mouth, and trotted off with Lucky in search of more challenging terrain. He felt his stomach turn over and his shoulders tighten as he picked up speed going down the hill Lucky had picked. "Help!" he yelped, "How do I stop this thing?"

Lucky was howling with laughter as Boris whizzed by him looking like he had just seen a ghost.

"That was cool!" Boris exclaimed after he managed to jump off the board without crashing into the trees at the bottom of the hill. He swaggered back to Lucky with a proud look in his eyes and a little smirk on his face.

"That was just a mole hill," scoffed Lucky, who noticed Boris's smug air. "Let me show you what real skateboarding looks like."

Lucky and Boris huffed and puffed up the steep incline of a giant hill. Carrying the board in their mouths made panting more difficult. When they reached the top, they could see for miles.

"No way!" Boris protested when Lucky challenged him to ride to the bottom of the hill. He could see that the road ended at the lake. "I'll be going a hundred miles per hour when I reach the bottom with no way to stop. What am I supposed to do, use the skateboard as a ski when I reach the water?"

Lucky just laughed and took the board. "Let me show you the way."

He placed the board on the road, jumped on, and took off like a missile down the steep hill. Boris noticed that Lucky curved back and forth on the hill to keep his speed down, but he had no idea how Lucky was able to control the board so well. The skateboarding dog reached the bottom, safe and sound.

Boris felt the lump growing in his throat as he saw Lucky struggling back up the hill with his skateboard. He wondered if that lump also had something to do with the fact that this was the place he had been dropped off by his former owner over seven years ago. When he reached the top, Lucky collapsed on the ground to recover from the long climb. He was panting hard as he enjoyed the sun on his head, the breeze on his fur, and the cocky feeling inside from his thrilling and triumphant ride.

"Okay, Boris. It's your turn," he said after gathering his breath.

Boris swallowed hard. "I—I can't do that," Boris resisted. "The hill is too steep, and I don't know how to turn or even how to stop."

"You'll never know until you try," Lucky taunted him.

Boris remembered how nervous he was whenever he watched Liam and Aidan skateboard down this hill. Liam always kept perfect control of the board and made steady turns all the way down the hill. Boris recalled how he admired Liam's skill and form as he made the ride look easy. Then he cringed as he remembered Aidan jumping on the board and racing fearlessly straight down the hill and, since he couldn't stop, going right into the lake with a huge splash. Boris trembled at the thought of Aidan's crashing, but he knew that the boy had had to learn the difference between thrill seeking and risk taking. Aidan had come out of the lake laughing, and Boris had eagerly licked his face, relieved that he hadn't been hurt.

"What are you waiting for?" Lucky prodded.

Boris threw caution to the wind and jumped on the board. He had a look of gleeful terror on his face as he quickly picked up speed and zoomed down the hill. He was wearing a big, toothy grin, his eyes looked like two moons, and his ears stuck up perfectly straight as the wind blew harder in his face with each roll of the wheels.

All of a sudden, Boris lost his balance, fell off the board, and went rolling into the sand along the side of the road. He ended up flat on his back in a bunch of tall weeds.

Lucky raced down the hill to check on his friend. "Are you all right?" he asked nervously.

Boris felt a little foolish but was relieved when he was able to move all his paws. "Just a few scrapes and bruises," he responded weakly.

Lucky fetched the board and returned to Boris. "I guess we left out a few steps," Lucky said sheepishly, feeling guilty that he had pushed Boris to take a risk he wasn't ready for.

"No problem," said Boris as he began to limp back home alongside Lucky. "It was fun, but I think I need more practice."

As they approached the Hamm fam's house, thoughts entered Boris's mind. "Maybe I need to work on taking fewer risks in my thrill seeking," he mused. "But I should certainly practice more with this board. Some day it could come in handy in my search for my brothers and sisters."

Guide for Chapter 30:

▼

Boris Shows Compassion

In this story, Boris learns to suspend judgment until he has looked below the surface.

In preparation for this conversation, reflect upon a situation in which you were the "different" one in a group.

This story deals with the ways in which we make initial judgments before finding out who a person is. It suggests that in order to be a more compassionate person, there are at least four things we shouldn't do:

➤ Don't judge a book by its cover.

➤ Don't be small in heart, mind, or soul.

➤ Don't let stereotypes close your mind.

➤ Don't be harder on others than you are on yourself.

There have been many times in my experience that I have let stereotypes influence the way I perceived people from different backgrounds and experiences than mine. I grew up in a small, rural, predominantly white, Midwestern town in which I heard many hateful, prejudicial, and disparaging remarks about people of color and people with nonstandard sexual orientations or religious beliefs. Not having anyone to present another point of view, at times I said things and acted in ways that now I feel ashamed about. Over the years, I have learned to own my privilege and prejudices. Hopefully, I have moved from intolerant to tolerant, from tolerant to accepting, and from accepting to welcoming. I have found that I have enriched my life immeasurably by seeking out differences instead of avoiding them in my life.

I have also learned that it is easier "not to do" than it is "to do." Not being mean is easier than being compassionate. Not being judgmental is easier than having an open mind and an open heart. That's why the themes in this story all start with "don't" instead of "do."

As a result of responding to this story, you might find yourself engaged with the child in any or all of these questions:

- Have you judged a person by their appearance, only to find out later how wrong you were?

- Is there a time when you have been "the different one" in the group? How did it feel?

- What's the difference between being tolerant and being accepting, welcoming, or inviting?

- Is it easier for you to find faults in others than to find them in yourself? Why?

CHAPTER 30

▼

BORIS SHOWS COMPASSION

"Hey, Boris, let me introduce you to Rodney, the new dog on the block," Gabby called out as she trotted into the Hamm family's yard with a strange-looking companion.

Rodney was a skinny mutt with short, spiky hair and a scrunched-up nose that Boris thought was ugly. "Nice to meet you," Boris managed to spit out, not really covering the immediate disdain he had for his new neighbor's appearance.

Gabby gave Boris a quick scowl. "Rodney and his family, the Vlads, just moved here from Russia," Gabby added cheerfully, trying to soften the harshness of Boris's cold greeting and to make Rodney feel comfortable. She saw that Rodney had dipped his scrawny head, and his ear had begun to twitch.

Feeling the heat of Gabby's glare, Boris shook himself all over and started again. "Welcome to the neighborhood, Rodney. What sort of games did you play in Russia?" he inquired with genuine interest.

Gabby smiled when she noticed that Rodney's ear had quit twitching. His eyes brightened, his tail started wagging, and his spiky hair appeared to rest more smoothly on his back. "Olgathon is my favorite!" Rodney replied enthusiastically. "In it, whoever swims upstream in a raging river for the longest time wins."

"Sounds exhausting to me," Boris said, remembering how tired he would get after even a brief dip in the lake. "There are some big rapids in rivers not far from here. Maybe my family, the Hamms, will take us to one so I can see how you do it," Boris suggested with a clear note of skepticism in his voice.

Gabby rolled her eyes at Boris and shook her head. "Well, Rodney, let's head down the road and see what Lucky and Prudence are up to," she said, and she and Rodney went on their way.

"Later," Boris mumbled. He slouched back to his house, feeling upset because he knew Gabby was mad at him for not being more gracious in welcoming Rodney to town. Gabby was so good at accepting the obvious and the subtle differences between Rodney and the dogs who lived in the neighborhood.

"Rats," Boris grumbled under his breath. "Rodney is going to ruin the whole neighborhood." In truth, Boris was feeling worried that Gabby would have less time for him, and he also felt small because he was being selfish and not particularly kind to Rodney.

After moping for a few minutes on the porch and feeling sorry for himself, Boris dragged himself up to his feet and out of his foul mood. "I need to talk to Zelda," he said to himself as he started to trot down to the pond.

Zelda saw Boris approach the pond with less zip than he normally exhibited. "What's troubling you, Boris?" she asked kindly.

After Boris shared the whole story of Russian Rodney ruining relationships with his friends, Zelda thought for a few moments before responding firmly. "Boris, I understand you feel worried that Rodney will disrupt the comfortable patterns you have with your friends. You also feel bad because you were rude. While you might not like to hear it, I think you are looking for the specks in Rodney's eye when you can't see the log in your own."

"What? I don't have a log in my eye. What's that supposed to mean?" Boris protested.

"It means you find it easier to see faults in others than it is to find them in yourself," Zelda explained. "You need to look for what you have in common rather than focus on what your differences may be. You also need to accept the weaknesses of others more than your own."

After a long pause in which Boris let the shock of what Zelda had said sink in, Boris replied thoughtfully, "I know you're right, Zelda. I'm quick to find the faults in others and slow to find my own faults, and I'm easier on myself than I am on others. But how do I change that?"

Boris appeared earnest in his desire to be a better dog. "You've already taken the first step," Zelda said, smiling with encouragement and fondness for her friend. "You have taken responsibility for your behavior."

Boris trotted back home along the trail with more pep than he had had on the way to the lake. He was once again grateful to have someone like Zelda to talk to about the things that made his tail curl under his legs.

As he emerged from the woods, Boris saw his friends bouncing down the street. He put it into high gear and raced down the street to catch up, kicking up a cloud of dust behind him. When he reached them, he dug his paws into the ground and skidded to a halt.

Lucky and Prudence greeted Boris enthusiastically. "Hey, where have you been?" "We missed you!" "Have you met Rodney?" they alternated.

Gabby chimed in more cautiously. "Yes, I introduced Rodney and Boris this morning."

Rodney glanced nervously at Boris, not quite sure what to expect him to say.

"Yeah!" Boris said brightly, setting aside his earlier, hasty first impression of the newcomer. "Rodney has some great new games to teach us!"

Rodney's anxious expression changed into a grin. The new friends continued down the road, getting to know each other.

Guide for Chapter 31:

▼

Boris Takes the Initiative

In this story, Boris learns that success requires both opportunity and initiative.

In preparation for this conversation, think about the opportunities you have had in your life that have made it possible for you to be successful.

This story deals with the two fundamental factors of successful development of one's character:

➢ Creating the conditions that enable you to advance on your quest for personal improvement

➢ Seizing opportunities when they arise

In my experience, I've had to take the initiative often to get what I wanted out of life. When I was in Vietnam, a friend of mine suggested that I establish a pen-pal relationship with a woman he knew who was spending her junior year in Paris. After a year of correspondence, this woman met me in California when I returned from the war, and we were married a year later. I took the initiative to make that relationship happen by continuing to write, by inviting her to meet me in California, and by taking every opportunity I could to see her. How different my life would have been otherwise.

As a result of responding to this story, you might find yourself engaged with the child in any or all of these questions:

• What does success mean to you?

- What opportunities have you taken advantage of in your life? Can you think of opportunities you have missed?

- Have you ever caused something to happen that wouldn't have if you hadn't taken the initiative?

- Do you know anyone who really has a way of making things happen?

CHAPTER 31

▼

BORIS TAKES THE INITIATIVE

Boris felt cramped. He thought he needed more space—a place where he could just get away and relax. It wasn't as though he didn't enjoy being in the Hamm house. He loved to play with Aidan and Liam, and life there was very comfortable. He had just celebrated his eighth anniversary with the Hamms, and he still felt very lucky to have found them.

Still, it seemed that every time he wanted to lie down and take a nap, Aidan would run across the room as fast as he could, slide on his socks on the slippery, wood floors, and throw his arms around Boris as he made his crash landing. If Aidan wasn't running around the house like a wild man, Liam would want to read a story to Boris. Boris loved to hear Liam read, but sometimes he preferred to have a little peace and quiet. After all, he was getting older—in human years, he was in his midfifties.

Boris felt like he was making progress on trying to improve himself, but having a place to go to collect his thoughts would definitely help him. Sure, he had his doghouse in the backyard, but whenever he settled into it, Lucky would come bouncing over and want to go for a swim. Just like he loved his family, Boris loved his friends, but they didn't help any in terms of giving him some private time to reflect.

"I've got it!" Boris said to himself as he was taking his daily walk on the trail through the woods. "I'll build a private cabin next to the stream."

It was his favorite spot; he loved the way the clearing opened up there, the way the light burst through the trees, and the soothing sounds of the stream. Boris sat down by the gently flowing water and thought about how he could build his retreat without anyone knowing. If Liam, Aidan, or Boris's pals found out, it would soon become a clubhouse instead of a sanctuary.

"Let's see," Boris mused, "I don't have a hammer and nails, I don't have any wood, and I don't have the skills I need to build the house." Any ordinary dog would have given up on the spot, but Boris was no ordinary dog. "I'll figure out a way to make this happen," he told himself resolutely, trying to muster the energy to get moving.

The first step, he decided, was to look around him for anything that would be of use. He realized that there was plenty of timber—sticks and branches covered the nearby forest floor. His eyebrows rose, and his ears perked up as he felt an energy surge in his body. Boris sprang into action, racing around finding the heaviest branches he could carry and putting them into a neat pile by the stream. Before long, he had stacked up fifty limbs.

He sat down, panting from exhaustion after his frantic rush to collect all the wood for his cabin. "Hmm," he thought, "how am I going to transform a pile of sticks into a secret hideaway?"

An idea flashed in his mind. Boris saw four trees standing closely together that formed a square of sorts. "I could make the four trees the corners of my house and use the branches for the sides," he concluded, feeling proud for being so creative and resourceful. "But how am I going to secure the branches and make them the right lengths?" A frown crossed his face. "I know!" he beamed as he sped back to the Hamm house.

Boris quietly snuck into the garage and found a hammer, some nails, and a saw. He used his mouth to put all the tools into Aidan's wagon, then he silently crept out of the garage, down the trail, and back to his pile of sticks, pulling the wagon in tow.

Boris measured the distance between the first two trees and sawed ten branches to that length. He then took the hammer and nailed the branches to the trees. He did the same for two more sides. "I think I'll leave one side open," he decided, as every muscle in his body was screaming for him to rest.

"Oops!" Boris exclaimed out loud when he noticed his house did not have a roof. "I didn't think about that," he thought with an embarrassed grin on his face. Boris really wanted to find a solution to this problem before the next time it might rain, so he thought very hard.

"Ah hah!" Boris leapt into the air with a spinning twirl. "I know! I'll just put some branches on top and cover them with leaves."

Boris completed this last step and went inside to relax within his newly created retreat. After a few moments in his quiet space, he remembered he needed to return the tools before they were discovered missing. With a satisfied bounce in his step, Boris wheeled the tools back to the garage and put them back where he had found them, including Aidan's wagon, making sure no one saw him in the act.

Boris heaved a big sigh, slowly wandered over to the porch, and took a well-earned nap. That day he had thought of a problem, come up with a solution, and implemented it. "It's good to take the initiative," Boris thought as he drifted asleep.

Guide for Chapter 32:

▼

Boris Suffers a Loss

In this story, Boris learns how to deal with the death of a friend.

In preparation for this conversation, reflect upon the friends and family members you have lost and the ways in which you keep their memories alive.

This story deals with the inevitability of death. It discusses how we can take this dreadful negative and turn it into something positive. The major themes are:

➤ Keeping memories alive

➤ Telling the whole truth about a person's life

➤ Dealing with the reality of our mortality

➤ Living with death on your shoulder

➤ Transforming dark events into happier ones

Death has delivered some devastating blows in my life's experience. I've lost a seventeen-year-old cousin to cancer; a seventeen-year-old nephew to suicide; friends to war, accidents, and disease; and both parents to old age. Each loss caused me terrible sadness and showed me great humility regarding the fragility of life. I have tried to be grateful for the impossible improbability of each day of life. Each person's death has inspired me to live as fully as possible.

When I lost my parents, I eulogized them in their fullness. Neither of them was perfect—both had faults. And both were amazing gifts to me and to many others.

Death comes into our lives in unpredictable ways. Some kids are exposed to it when they are very young, and others don't experience loss until later in life. This story attempts to present the realities and possibilities of death without being heavy-handed.

As a result of responding to this story, you might find yourself engaged with the child in any or all of these questions:

- What was the greatest loss you have ever experienced?

- How do you keep alive the memories of someone you have lost?

- Have you been able to find something useful and positive in a death?

CHAPTER 32

▼

BORIS SUFFERS A LOSS

Boris had never had to deal with death before. Then one otherwise normal day, he heard from Gabby that Paul Pitt had been hit by a car and killed. The news made Boris terribly sad. Even though Paul and Boris had had their differences, Boris took Paul's death very hard.

"I just can't believe it," Boris said. "It seems so strange that we were playing ball with Paul yesterday, and now he's gone."

"I know," Gabby responded. "It feels awful. It's so hard to lose a friend."

Boris hung his head and walked with heavy paws back to his house. He went inside, lay down, and thought about all of his memories of Paul, both good and bad. "Paul was far from perfect," Boris thought to himself. "His growling was intimidating, his grumpiness put me off, and he played too rough. Even so, Paul always stuck up for his friends, spoke honestly, and he even signed up for a few of my clubs." As difficult as Paul was at times, Boris knew he was going to miss him.

As Boris reflected on Paul's life and their friendship, Prudence stopped by to share her grief and to lend her support. "It was meant to be," Prudence suggested in a soothing tone.

Boris frowned. "I don't believe that things are meant to be; I think they just happen and you have to deal with them," he replied sadly.

"Oh, Boris, I know you don't agree, but I believe there is a reason for everything."

"I have a hard time thinking there is a good reason for Paul being killed instantly by a car, or for a lot of other terrible things that happen in this world," Boris replied calmly and kindly.

"I guess it's okay to disagree on whether or not there is a reason, but we both feel horrible that this accident happened, and we both feel the pain of this sudden loss," Prudence said. She and Boris fell silent for a while and simply took comfort in just being together.

Soon after Prudence left, Zelda stopped by to let Boris know she was thinking about him. "Is there any way I can be helpful?" she wanted to know.

"How can I make any sense out of this, Zelda?" Boris asked as a tear fell down his face.

"I'm not sure you can, Boris," Zelda sighed. "Sometimes bad things happen for no good reason. It's hard to deal with a death like this, but it can make you realize how precious life is. For some dogs, a death shocks them into being more grateful for every day they have on this earth. And it connects them to every other being: we all are born, we live, and we die. Understanding that fact creates compassion for others."

Zelda paused, and Boris nodded to show his understanding. She went on, "There are also those who become bitter, though. It's just another choice we have to make. It's not easy to find anything good about pain, I know. But try to ask yourself how you can transform this pain and darkness into something useful."

Boris and Zelda sat in silence for a long time. Finally, Boris said, "Maybe we should put a sign in the road that says, "Dogs at Play—Please Slow Down."

Zelda nodded solemnly. "I think that's a good idea, Boris. It won't bring Paul back, but it will help us remember him and might even make this road a safer place for all of us."

GUIDE FOR CHAPTER 33:

▼

BORIS DISCOVERS THE IMPORTANCE OF DOUBT

In this story, Boris learns that issues are seldom as clear as black and white and that gray areas are predominant in life.

In preparation for this conversation, reflect upon the times in your life when you were convinced you were absolutely right ... until it turned out you were not. Was the issue really as clear-cut as you thought it was?

This story discusses how Boris let the stereotype about another race of dogs blind him to the individual variations that are inevitable with each dog. Several truth-seeking themes are introduced in this story:

➢ Embracing uncertainty

➢ Conducting good research

➢ Seeking out multiple sources

➢ Creating a balanced perspective

➢ Resisting generalizations

In my experience, I have run across many people who have held strict black-or-white beliefs with little room for tolerance or open-mindedness of other ideas. For example, I have found that many religious teachings see the world as black or white. Either you subscribe to a set of teachings or you are shut out of various possibilities for life and death. For me, the literal interpretation of religious teachings limits the rich meaning underlying so much of the very texts they uphold.

In studying the major religions of the world, I have discovered that many of them have esoteric splinter groups: Islam has Sufism, Judaism has the Kabbalah, and Christianity has Gnosticism. Among these more mystical subsets, there is a high level of convergence in thinking and beliefs. All of them encourage a person to live in the layers of life instead of the literal word. All of these teachings, religious or otherwise, challenge students to look deeply inside and to find their own truth. They are less interested in dogma and creed and more interested in possibilities. It is my belief that this acceptance that life contains gray areas is an overall better philosophical approach to take in all aspects of life, not just religion.

As a result of responding to this story, you might find yourself engaged with the child in any or all of these questions:

- What beliefs of yours are you absolutely certain of? On what evidence do you base those beliefs?

- Have you ever taken time to research an area in which you have strong beliefs?

- Do you know anyone who does not act in ways you might expect them to act based on their appearance? For example, have you found that looks don't always tell the whole story? Or, have you ever simply trusted appearances when you could have looked more deeply for the truth?

CHAPTER 33

▼

BORIS DISCOVERS THE IMPORTANCE OF DOUBT

Boris felt absolutely certain he was right. Not only had he heard Liam and Aidan talking about how all Dobermans were mean, but Lucky and Gabby had also shared their experiences with him. Boris knew beyond a shadow of doubt that the entire gang of Dobermans in the next town could not be trusted.

"Have you ever met a Doberman?" Prudence asked when Boris shared with her his fears about this particular breed of dog.

"Well, not really," he stammered, "but I've heard stories about how mean they are and how they will attack you without warning if you wander into their territory."

"Who told you these stories, and have you read anything about them?" Prudence politely inquired.

"I haven't really read much, but everything I hear makes me glad we don't have any Dobermans in our neighborhood," Boris replied defensively, realizing that his certainty might not be entirely well-founded. He was beginning to doubt the absolute confidence with which he had started this conversation.

"Let's look up Dobermans on Dogipedia and see what we can find out," Prudence suggested as she started to trot off to her Internet-enabled doghouse. With her high-speed cable, it took only a few seconds to get the information they were looking for in the Dogipedia entry:

Doberman Pinschers are, in general, a gentle, loyal, loving, and highly intelligent breed. Although there is variation in temperament, a typical pet Doberman attacks only if it has been mistreated or believes that it, its property, or its family are in danger. The Doberman Pinscher is less frequently involved in attacks on humans resulting in fatalities than several other dog breeds. Those familiar with the breed consider well-bred and properly socialized Doberman Pinschers to be excellent pets and companions, suitable for families with other dog breeds, excellent with young children, and even cats. The modern Doberman Pinscher is well known as a loyal and devoted family member. The Doberman has been used as a protection and guard dog, due to its intelligence, loyalty, and ability to physically challenge aggressors. Doberman Pinschers were once commonly used in police work and in the military. They are often seen in movies and video games as being aggressive, so many people are afraid of the breed.

"Yikes," Boris exclaimed, feeling silly that he was so sure of himself though he was only basing his opinion on the stories of two children without doing any of his own research.

"If you are really interested, you should go to the library and read some books or talk to the dogs in the neighborhood where the Dobermans live," Prudence offered, knowing that Dogipedia was not a foolproof source of information, either.

"Or we could go find a Doberman who would talk to us," Boris continued the thought. "Doubt may be a better friend of truth than certainty."

"I like that saying, Boris. I think it means you are more likely to find the truth if you challenge ideas, right?" Prudence asked.

Boris nodded, then he spotted another friend. "Hey, Lucky," he called out, "do you want to come with Prudence and me to talk to a few Dobermans in the next town?"

"No way!" Lucky quickly yelped with a horrified look on his face. "It's been nice knowing you," he added, looking at Boris and Prudence like they had lost their minds.

Boris and Prudence just shrugged—as well as a dog can shrug, anyway—and trotted down the road in search for the truth about Dobermans. At least, they sought a more balanced and objective view of the breed. Before long, they saw some friendly looking dogs. "Do you know of any Dobermans in the area we might be able to talk to?" Prudence asked hopefully.

"Sure," one of the dogs replied, "Damian Doberman lives up on the hill in that red farmhouse." Then he advised, "He's protective of the kids who live there, though, so don't rush in and surprise him."

"Thanks," Prudence and Boris said a little nervously as they resumed climbing the hill to the farmhouse.

Prudence spotted him first. Damian was a big, lean, brown dog with a sharp, pointed nose. He approached Boris and Prudence with his ears straight up and its tail pointed back.

"Hi, Damian," Prudence greeted nervously.

"We wondered if we might be able to talk to you," Boris said with a friendly tone in his voice as he noticed the rippling muscles of the Doberman's back and legs.

Damian assessed the visitors. "Come on in," he replied after determining in his own sharp mind that Prudence and Boris were not threats. "What's on your mind?"

They all sat down under a shady tree and began their conversation.

"I was wondering what it was like to be a Doberman," Boris asked. "Does everyone shy away from you?"

Damian looked at Prudence and Boris with kind, understanding eyes. "At first, yes, people are very cautious and approach me nervously. When I move toward them slowly and lick their hand, though, they quickly relax. Other dogs, like yourselves, seem to be able to see more quickly that just because I look the way I do doesn't mean I'm ferocious."

Prudence replied honestly, "I must admit, I was a little scared when I first saw you, but I noticed right away that you were friendly."

The trio of dogs spent a little longer discussing stereotypes and generally talking about living a dog's life. Together they found common ground despite their differences in breeding.

"I can understand how Dobermans might frighten people," Boris said to Prudence as they started their trek back down the hill and home.

"They do look strong and intimidating," Prudence responded, "and they have been known to hurt people if they have been treated badly or if they think they are being threatened."

"Yeah, but Damian was really friendly, and I enjoyed getting to know him. I guess it's not true that all Dobermans are bad," Boris concluded, feeling good that he had made the effort to expand his understanding.

Prudence replied, "I think the best we can do is to be open to the possibilities of building relationships with all types of dogs, regardless of their reputations."

"Yes, I think you're right," Boris agreed.

GUIDE FOR CHAPTER 34:

▼

BORIS LIGHTENS UP

In this story, Boris learns how to let go of a negative emotion.

In preparation for this conversation, think about a time in your life when you were not only in a bad mood, but you hung onto the mood and wallowed in it.

This story demonstrates how easily and quickly we can slip from feelings of euphoria to a blue funk as a result of the simplest setbacks. Two key themes for staying positive are covered in the story:

➤ Observing your mood

➤ Letting go of negative emotions

In my experience, the key to avoiding bad moods is to notice quickly where your feelings are headed before you get in too deep. In their work on self-defeating behaviors, psychologists have discovered that the quicker we realize we are on a path that can only produce negative results, the easier it is to get off that path. As we stay on the path longer, our negativity gains momentum, and it is harder to turn it around. To make the choice to let go of a bad mood early, we need to have a high level of self-awareness and a willingness to let go of those feelings and thoughts that will only defeat ourselves. I have found that dwelling on the negative or what's unfair in life does not help anyone, and it makes it more likely that I will not accomplish my goals, as well.

As a result of responding to this story, you might find yourself engaged with the child in any or all of these questions:

- When do you get in a bad mood?

- Is there a specific event that can trigger a negative mood in you?

- When do you first notice that you are grumpy?

- How do you let go of that grumpy feeling?

- Can you think of a time when have you decided to wallow in a bad feeling instead of letting it go? What was the result?

CHAPTER 34

▼

BORIS LIGHTENS UP

Boris was so angry with himself. Gabby, Prudence, and he had planned an overnight getaway to celebrate Lucky's tenth birthday. This was a big event because reaching the ten-year mark in a dog's life is a major milestone. Boris was excited all week because this was going to be a surprise party for Lucky.

Lucky was thrilled when Boris, Prudence, and Gabby suddenly appeared at his house and said, "Pack your bags, Lucky. We're going to a fancy dog retreat to celebrate your birthday." Lucky was so happy he did three flips and licked his friends vigorously. Prudence was a little put-off by the licking, but she tolerated it anyway.

Quickly, they packed their bags and headed out. After three miles of strenuous walking over the hills and through the weeds, Boris realized that he had forgotten his toothbrush. Suddenly the mood of the whole excursion went from happy and gleeful to sour and sullen.

"I hate to forget things," Boris muttered, "and I can't get started in the morning without brushing my teeth. Besides, I'll have bad breath, and none of you will want to be around me." Boris continued to mumble and grumble as he stumbled over a log he hadn't seen on the path.

"We could turn back," Prudence suggested.

"Or we could all chip in and buy you another one," Gabby chimed in.

"You could use mine," Lucky offered.

"Eww, how gross!" they all said in unison at the birthday dog's solution.

"I don't know what to do," Boris responded, still mad at himself for making this silly mistake.

"What would Zelda say?" Prudence asked, trying to be helpful.

Boris thought for a minute. "She'd probably say, 'Why don't you see this as an opportunity to practice letting go and just lightening up a little,'" Boris replied, laughing quietly at how Zelda's simple wisdom sometimes made a profound difference in how he viewed his life.

"Makes sense to me," Gabby added, nodding in agreement and impressed that Boris was able to anticipate what Zelda might say.

"Okay, I'll give it a try," Boris promised, even though he still smarted from making his stupid mistake.

After a few hours of hiking, they arrived at the retreat. "There it is!" Gabby barked excitedly with her tail wagging wildly.

"It's so beautiful," Prudence exclaimed when she saw the retreat. The most luxurious doghouses she had ever seen spread out in front of their eyes.

"What a great birthday present!" Lucky said, his eyes wide open with amazement as he surveyed all the dog toys in the huge play area.

Boris just smiled. Not only was he pleased that their idea for the event was such a success, but he was also proud of himself for not letting his mistake ruin a terrific party. He took a deep breath and let it go, no longer worrying about something as small as forgetting a toothbrush.

GUIDE FOR CHAPTER 35:

▼

BORIS ADJUSTS HIS EXPECTATIONS

In this story, Boris learns to laugh at himself.

In preparation for this conversation, reflect upon the times in your life in which you took yourself too seriously. What was the cause? Was it really justified?

This story describes how Boris fell into a depressed state because he had set a bunch of unrealistic goals and then beat himself up when he didn't accomplish them. He believed that the world only rewards "doing," not "being," and that he could only reward himself for doing extraordinary, if not impossible, tasks. There are two themes in this story:

➤ Learning to set realistic goals

➤ Being able to laugh at yourself

In my experience, goal setting is essential for personal development. Goals should neither be too high nor too low. They should be based on an objective assessment of your capability, your commitment, and the culture in which you live, learn, and work. One of my daughters and I share a vulnerability of setting unrealistic goals. After her first tennis lesson, Rebecca decided she wanted to play at Wimbledon. She might have been living in a culture that rewarded achievement and provided opportunities, but I knew she had neither the commitment nor the capability to achieve that goal.

As an author, I always expected my books to receive rave reviews and to become best sellers. Over the years, though, I have learned to set more modest goals for my books and to laugh at any delusional thoughts that may creep into my head about wildly optimistic sales. On the flip side, I know some extremely talented young people who set their goals too low and thus limit the probability of their seizing the amazing opportunities that might otherwise present themselves along the path of life.

As a result of responding to this story, you might find yourself engaged with the child in any or all of these questions:

- What are your goals? How realistic are they?

- What happens when someone challenges one of your goals or you don't achieve it? Do you learn from the experience, or do you get defensive and down on yourself?

- How easy is it for you to laugh at yourself? Can you accept the fact that we are all idiots in our own ways, and that's just part of being human?

CHAPTER 35

▼

BORIS ADJUSTS HIS EXPECTATIONS

Boris was discouraged. He had tried to pull off a flawless performance at the latest dance contest, and he had failed. His triple twirl with a flip at the end had fallen short of the mark, and he had come in second in the competition.

Boris had tried to be the perfect pet, but he kept dropping the paper in the mud or forgetting to shake off all the leaves from his back before he went inside. He had tried to sit patiently with Liam when he was reading his book, but he kept getting restless and jumping into the boy's lap, disturbing his concentration.

Boris always tried to write the perfect speech for his School of Possibilities lessons, but he noticed that many dogs were still falling asleep during his lectures.

"Boris, I enjoy your visits," Zelda said, "but you've been coming out to see me every day for the last month."

"I'm such a flawed dog," he replied with his head hanging down and his ears drooping. "Nothing I do is good enough."

"Good enough for whom?" Zelda asked, wondering if Boris was setting his goals too high or if the people around him were setting unrealistic standards for him.

"Good enough for me!" he exclaimed.

"Ahh," Zelda sighed as she nodded her head. With a twinkle in her eyes, she prodded, "And what makes you think you should be perfect in everything you do?"

"Because I'm Boris the Wonder Dog," Boris giggled, realizing that he had been taking himself entirely too seriously. "I can do anything—even fly!"

Boris started laughing so hard he couldn't contain himself. "I'm even thinking about becoming a skateboarding professional," Boris continued, staying in the spirit of poking fun at himself. Soon he was rolling on the ground laughing at his silliness.

"Boris, you're a very talented dog," Zelda said reassuringly, "but sometimes your ambition and goals exceed your talent. You need to adjust your expectations a bit. I'm all for pursuing one's possibilities, but you may want to consider calling yourself Mr. *Im*possibility," she chided gently, joining in the laugh fest.

"Thanks, Zelda, for bringing me back to reality," Boris said. He was still chuckling to himself as he trotted back home with a lighter step than he'd had just minutes before.

As Boris crossed over the bridge on the trail and came out into the clearing, he saw Lucky looking for him in the Hamm yard. "Hey, Lucky. What's up?" he called out as he pranced lightheartedly into the yard.

"I was thinking I might sign up for the Iron Dog Triathlon," Lucky said, his tail wagging furiously.

"You can't be serious!" Boris replied, grinning doggishly. "I would never set a goal that high for myself."

"Hah! Look who is talking," Lucky retorted. "You're the king of unrealistic goals."

They both laughed at each other and at themselves.

GUIDE FOR CHAPTER 36:

▼

BORIS LEARNS TO APPRECIATE DIFFERENCES

In this story, Boris learns to value differences and to modify his style ... occasionally.

In preparation for this conversation, think about the personal preferences of your best friends. Do they approach life in similar ways to you or in different ways?

This story specifies a variety of ways that differentiate style preferences. It illustrates the differences between people who are reserved versus outgoing, indirect versus direct, calm or steady versus urgent, and detail oriented versus big-picture oriented. The key themes in this story are:

➢ Viewing individual differences as gifts

➢ Flexing your personal style

In my experience, in order to make interpersonal relations go well, it is important to know yourself and to know others. One part of knowing yourself and others is being able to identify your style preferences. At home, I am reserved, direct, urgent, and big-picture oriented. At work, I am more outgoing, but still prefer a direct, urgent, and strategic approach to getting a job done.

I sometimes run into conflicts when I am too direct or too decisive. Some people are put off by my blunt feedback, and others prefer not to rush decisions or implementation. I have learned to assess the preferences of the people with whom I work and to calibrate my sense of urgency to the cultural norms in which I am working. I have also learned to make sure I collaborate with people who are more detail oriented, diplomatic, and cautious than I am. That way, our styles complement each other. Thankfully, my wife is a thorough, thoughtful, deliberate decision maker. I've learned to trust her guidance on some of my more impulsive, and potentially misguided, ideas.

As a result of responding to this story, you might find yourself engaged with the child in any or all of these questions:

- What are your preferences for relating to people and getting work done? Do you tend to be more direct or diplomatic? Are you more reserved or outgoing? Do you prefer a slow, steady pace, or do you push for action?

- How do you react to people with different relating or learning preferences? Do you get irritated? Are you able to modify your style to accommodate their preferences?

- Do you seek out and respect differences in others?

CHAPTER 36

▼

BORIS LEARNS TO APPRECIATE DIFFERENCES

Boris was grumpy. All his friends had different preferences for the ways they liked to live, learn, and play. He couldn't understand why everyone didn't like to do things the way he did. After all, Boris's style worked for him … most of the time.

Gabby was the diplomat of the neighborhood. She liked to state her ideas carefully and persuade others tactfully. Gabby would rather "ask" than "tell" and presented her ideas modestly, sometimes even understating them.

Boris, on the other hand, loved to bark out his ideas candidly and boldly. He would try to influence other dogs with an assertive, direct approach and could come across as overly self-confident and forceful. He was comfortable confronting conflicts and debating differences. He loved taking charge and giving directions to the point of annoying his friends.

"Hey, Boris," Gabby might say, "what would you think about reading a book about cats for our next book club meeting?"

"Cats? Why would a bunch of dogs want to read about cats? I want to read about the dog that loved to sneak up on deer in the woods and scare them into bouncing away," Boris would respond enthusiastically.

Prudence was the precision queen of the neighborhood. She loved details, clear plans, and specific guidelines. Prudence would only go forward on an idea when she thoroughly understood all the steps involved.

Boris, on the other hand, was always looking for innovative ways to reach goals. He loved unconventional ideas, open plans, and unpredictable results. He never read any directions before he embarked on one of his wild ideas, and he got frustrated when there were too many rules. Boris was more interested in picturing new possibilities than developing precise plans.

"Let's try to sail across the lake today," Boris might suggest to Prudence.

Prudence, looking horrified, would inquire, "Where can we find a boat?" How can we learn to hoist the sail? What can we use for life vests? Who will help us?"

Boris would roll his eyes, having no patience for all these irritating details, and bounce over to Lucky's. He would find fewer of those annoying obstacles there. Lucky and Boris both liked to take action and make decisions quickly. They liked fast-paced projects and loved games that required quick responses. Whenever an opportunity would arise, those two would jump all over it.

Sally Siamese, on the other hand, enjoyed a more leisurely pace. She liked to consider many options before deciding what to do. Sally got things done by sticking with it and persisting in her efforts. She was very cautious and preferred playing games that required a great deal of calculation and thought.

"Sally, what would you like to do this afternoon?" Boris would ask eagerly, barely able to contain his excitement.

"I don't know," Sally would respond, scratching her whiskers. "I was thinking about drawing, or looking for mushrooms, or sneaking up on birds, or …"

"Just let me know when you decide," Boris would interrupt, heaving a sigh of exasperation because Sally couldn't just make a decision and act.

Zelda always responded to other dogs in a quiet and reserved manner. She liked to interact with one dog at a time, and she kept her emotions private and contained. She preferred to think problems through and to clarify all the feelings involved. You could always count on Zelda to be reflective and to keep private information confidential.

Boris, on the other hand, shared his feelings freely. He loved lots of activity and preferred to talk through his problems more than think them through. Boris used many gestures and expressions when he talked with his friends, and he enjoyed the frequent contact with the other dogs and people in the neighborhood. Zelda was the dog he went to when he had a problem, but she was not the dog he'd ask to join him when he was up to some mischievous prank. And today, Boris was having a problem understanding all his friends' differences in style.

"Zelda, I'm so frustrated with Gabby, Prudence, and Sally," Boris began. "Gabby seems reluctant to tell me what she really thinks, Prudence drives me crazy with details, and Sally takes forever to decide what she wants to do. Lucky's the only one who can make a quick decision, but even he slows me down with his desire to please everyone."

"So you're really frustrated because your friends prefer to do things differently than you do," Zelda responded.

"Yes, exactly!" Boris said, wagging his tail because Zelda understood.

"What if you started viewing all of those differences as gifts instead of irritants?" Zelda asked.

"What do you mean?" Boris's tail stopped wagging.

"I mean, it's helpful to have a diplomat dog among your friends, like Gabby, and a detail dog like Prudence, and a steady cat like Sally. It's great that you are so direct, decisive, and expressive, but you could get yourself in a lot of trouble without dogs who pay attention to details, see things through, and are a little more subtle than you are."

Boris thanked Zelda and trotted back to the Hamm house, feeling a little stunned by what Zelda had told him. But then he started thinking about how boring life would be if all dogs looked like him, thought like him, and liked the same things he did. And he felt grateful that he had a dog like Zelda who definitely had different preferences than he had.

Boris wasn't so sure, though, how he was ever going to see all those irritating differences among his friends as gifts. He understood that other styles complemented his own and that his style may help those who are too deliberate actually make quicker progress on decisions. Still, he knew it would take work on his part to change his impulsive behaviors.

GUIDE FOR CHAPTER 37:

▼

BORIS FINDS THE COURAGE TO ACT

In this story, Boris has a defining moment.

In preparation for this conversation, reflect on a time in your life when you wished you had taken action, but you didn't. Conversely, think about a situation in which you stepped up and did what you needed to do to deal with a crisis.

This story presents a side of Boris we haven't seen before. It reveals the heroic side of Boris's personality and demonstrates that he has the courage to take charge when a situation calls for bold action. There is just one main theme in this story:

➢ Stepping up in a crisis

In my experience as a facilitator, I try to stay out of the way as much as possible. My goal is to design a meeting in which people feel productive, innovative, and free to express themselves honestly. At times, when the meeting goes off course or the conversation degenerates into a venting session, I intervene to elevate the conversation and focus the discussion.

As a father, I have always tried to free my children to be who they are. My goal was to support the pursuit of their dreams and passions, not to control their behavior to conform to my wishes. When I thought they were dancing on a dangerous edge or were engaged in destructive relationships, however, I did not hesitate to act.

In the book *The Kite Runner*, author Khaled Hosseini describes a boy who watches in despair as his friend is terribly abused by a group of thugs. The boy never forgives himself for not acting to help his friend. It was a defining moment for the boy that stayed with him for the rest of his life.

Defining moments can be for better or for worse. In times of crisis, some people find extraordinary courage that they did not know they had. Others discover debilitating cowardice when faced with a crisis. The problem is that you never really know until the crisis occurs.

As a result of responding to this story, you might find yourself engaged with the child in any or all of these questions:

- Can you think of an instance when were you able to find the courage to act when you saw a need for action?

- What kinds of situations in communities, and in countries as a whole, require members to put themselves at risk?

- When you think about your friends, which ones do you believe you could count on to help you if you were in trouble?

CHAPTER 37

▼

BORIS FINDS THE COURAGE TO ACT

It was 2:00 PM. The blazing, midafternoon sun had Boris searching for shade and longing for a cooler time.

"Let's go swimming!" Lucky yelled when he saw Boris stretching on his porch. "Sounds like a great idea," Boris responded enthusiastically.

Boris and Lucky trotted down the road, making stops to see if Sally, Gabby, or Prudence might join them.

"I can't decide," Sally said with a stumped looked on her feline face.

"It's a good idea," Gabby barked out, "but I don't want to leave my air-conditioned doghouse."

"How far are we going? Should I use sunblock? What should I wear?" Prudence asked, trying to get more details so she could plan the adventure.

Lucky and Boris looked at each other and shook the ears on their furry heads. They quickly fired back the answers: "Out to the raft. Yes—use SPF 30. Wear your little pink bikini."

"Ha ha, funny dogs," Prudence said as she rolled her eyes.

Boris and Lucky were nipping at each other's ears when Prudence caught up with them dressed in a dowdy, green suit that covered every inch of her curly fur.

"You would have been cooler in the pink one," Lucky teased as they continued down the road, thinking about how refreshing the cool lake would be.

As they turned the corner heading to the lake, the dog pack was nearly stampeded by a monstrous horse that suddenly thundered by them.

"Aidan, what are you doing on that horse?" Boris barked, worried that Aidan had once again crossed the line from risk taking to thrill seeking.

Liam was running behind as fast as could, calling out, "Slow down, Aidan! You're not sitting right in the saddle, and you're not holding tight enough to the reins."

The boys had just returned from the zoo, where Aidan had seen someone riding a camel. Aidan knew instantly that he wanted to ride a big animal, too, even if it didn't have a long neck. He'd figured it couldn't possibly be that hard to ride a horse. "All you have to do is jump on, kick him in the butt, and say giddyup!" Aidan had said confidently.

"How could you possibly believe that?" Mr. Hamm had said, trying desperately to take that wild idea out of Aidan's head but knowing that "hold that thought" was a foreign concept to the boy.

Liam's face turned brick red, and his blood had gone ice cold as he watched Aidan clinging for life to the back of the horse. Thinking quickly, Boris raced ahead of the horse and barked commandingly at it to stop. To everyone's surprise and relief, the horse came to a screeching halt. By that time Aidan was dangling over the horse's side with a firm grip on its mane and a wide smile on his face.

Liam came up to horse, puffing for air. He grabbed Aidan by the waist and lowered him to the ground. "Aidan, Aidan," Liam said. "What are we going to do with you?"

"That was fun!" the other boy screamed, delighting in the wild ride he had just taken. "You should try it!"

Boris returned to the corner where Prudence and Lucky had watched the whole scene with their jaws open.

"I think we really deserve a swim now," Lucky said, admiring the courage and quickness with which Boris had acted.

"First one in gets a bone," Prudence said, bolting off in a green streak to the lake.

After having their fill, they came splashing out of the lake. They all stopped to shake the water off their bodies. The people sunbathing nearby did not appreciate being sprayed by their vigorous shaking.

Lucky and Prudence noticed that Boris was trembling. "I guess that water was too cold for you, Boris," Prudence said. "You should have worn a suit like mine."

Boris nodded in agreement, but he knew inside that the trembling was not caused by the cold water. He had just realized how close he had come to being run over by a stampeding horse by taking the risk to save Aidan. Even so, Boris did feel proud because he had found the courage to act when he saw that Aidan was in trouble.

GUIDE FOR CHAPTER 38:

▼

BORIS PRACTICES DIPLOMACY

In this story, Boris learns how to find peaceful solutions.

In preparation for this conversation, reflect on the major conflicts you've had in your life and the way you were able to resolve those conflicts.

This story deals with humanity's long history of violence. It recognizes the problem of achieving peaceful solutions when evil lurks. The story presents two options for finding peace and harmony that have not been adequately tested. The first—setting the tone for diplomacy while mobilizing collective strength—is uncommon but fairly conventional. Meanwhile, the second—ending identification, beginning to collaborate, and continuing to send positive thoughts—is far more revolutionary. Four themes are covered in this story:

➢ Building a coalition of strength

➢ Leveraging individual strengths for the greater good

➢ Seeking peaceful solutions

➢ Maintaining a vigil for evil

In my experience as a soldier in Vietnam, I learned that war should be the option of last resort. I believe the wars in Korea, Vietnam, and the most recent Iraq war were not necessary. Peaceful solutions would have produced more productive and sustainable outcomes. We can't be naïve about the evil intentions of extremist groups, and we can be far more effective at building coalitions, leveraging strengths, and patiently seeking peaceful solutions.

As a result of responding to this story, you might find yourself engaged with the child in any or all of these questions:

- How have you managed conflicts you have had with your friends?

- How quickly are you tempted to engage in some act of violence or getting even as a way of settling a conflict?

- When were your friends able to solve a conflict without exchanging mean comments or hateful words? Is it more common to solve such problems peacefully? Does any benefit come from solving them forcefully?

CHAPTER 38

▼

BORIS PRACTICES DIPLOMACY

Boris couldn't believe his ninth anniversary with the Hamm fam had come and gone. Life was good for Boris at this point in his life. He had settled into a reasonable exercise program and was feeling fit. He was no Damian Doberman, but he had the energy to do what he wanted to do. His book club was going well, and he was continuing to learn.

Boris had lost some of the zeal he had once had for forming clubs and reforming the world, but he was feeling wiser and more centered than he had in his youth. Even though his tail wasn't constantly wagging and his body wasn't shaking every moment in anticipation of some new adventure, his ears still perked up when he heard a good idea, and his enthusiasm was still contagious. His relationships with the other dogs in the neighborhood had grown deeper, and he had learned to accept and value their differences. And Boris had drawn even closer to his wise friend, Zelda.

It's true that Boris had struggled through many life challenges. As a puppy, Boris had been overly rambunctious, overly confident, and overly active. He had taken himself too seriously, had tried to impose his thoughts on others, and was too caught up in being famous. Even though he never became the dancing dog diva, he still enjoyed dancing and was always looking for new moves. Even the thought of a championship still flashed through his active brain.

Overall, Boris was still on his quest for growth and still held hope in his heart that he would someday connect with his brothers and sisters. But right now, bigger challenges remained. Boris and his friends were having a meeting to discuss a looming threat.

"Boris, what do you think we should do about that Rogue Rascals gang in the next town?" Lucky asked nervously. "The attacks on other dogs keep getting closer to our neighborhood, and my nasty scar from when I was ambushed a few years ago reminds me that the same thing could happen to any of us at any time."

Boris shook his head sadly as he thought about the right action to take. "It's a hard problem," he said, deeply puzzled and concerned. "First, we need to organize all the dogs in our neighborhood so we can defend ourselves if the gang attacks. Second, we need to reach out to the packs in other neighborhoods to increase our collective strength. Then the rogue pack will know that any attack will be met with an immediate and overwhelming response. And third, we need to keep reaching out to the leader of the Rogue Rascals to figure out a way we can all live in peace. None of those is easy."

Gabby, Prudence, and Sally had been listening intently to this conversation, their shivering legs giving away their fear. "What if we held a summit," Gabby said, "to hear what every pack thinks we should do to help?"

"I think we need to develop a detailed plan," Prudence suggested. "That way everyone would know exactly what to do in case of an attack."

Sally thought long and hard. Finally, she said, "We could hold an animal art conference and invite everyone to contribute, including the Rogue Rascals."

Remembering his Interbarkem days when he went to dancing camp for dogs, Boris said, "Good idea, Sally. In the invitations we could say we are promoting animal friendship through the universal language of the arts."

Everyone nodded their furry heads in agreement, and Boris noticed that everyone's legs had stopped trembling, their jaws were not so clenched, and there were even a few wagging tails.

"Prudence, why don't you develop a plan? Sally, you can create the brochure. Gabby, maybe you could visit the friendly packs we already know, talk up the conference, and involve them in organizing it. And how about if Lucky and I make some initial contact with the Rogue Rascals? We'll see if they might want to come and how they might want to participate."

All the dogs barked approval, their ears perked up, and everyone went off to play their parts. Boris was left behind. He knew he would need to think carefully about how to provide adequate security for this conference.

Clearly, Boris had emerged as a leader in the neighborhood. He had grown steadily into the role, and the other dogs recognized that he had earned their respect and trust. They valued his perspective and his ability to think. Boris, though, still felt insecure in this role. He lumbered out to the woods where Zelda lived to see what she thought about his plan.

"Boris, those are good ideas. It sounds like everyone wants to get involved—that's a real plus. It may or may not work; I don't know," Zelda said, trying to support Boris's noble effort and still be honest.

"Well, what do you think it will take?" Boris reacted, somewhat disappointed by Zelda's less-than-full confidence in the plan.

Zelda reflected for a long time. Finally, she said, "My point of view may not be what you want to hear."

"Say it anyway," Boris pleaded, steeling himself for what he knew would be another challenge to conventional thinking.

"I believe there are three critical steps required to achieve some level of harmony and peace in our world."

"What are they?" Boris implored her, adding, "I want to hear them even if I don't agree."

Zelda looked deeply into Boris's eyes and said, "First, everyone needs to stop overidentifying with their particular belief systems. Second, we need to start working collaboratively to find creative solutions to the problems we are facing. That means we all work together to find the best idea. Third, everyone needs to do what they can to send positive energy into the universe. That means making a conscious and intentional effort to stop being negative and to think positive thoughts. Unfortunately, I don't have a lot of confidence that those steps will ever happen, because each of those steps is a revolution in itself."

Boris paused and reflected on what Zelda had said. "What do you mean when you say each step is a revolution, Zelda?"

"I mean that the steps I mentioned are not baby steps. They are giant steps that require great effort."

"You're probably right," Boris finally agreed. "But until that revolution occurs, we can only do what we can do."

They looked at each other for a long time before Boris nodded his head and trotted back to the Hamm house. He had work to do.

Guide for Chapter 39:

▼

Boris Celebrates
a Milestone

In this story, Boris summarizes what he has learned in his life and gives thanks for what he has.

In preparation for this conversation, reflect upon the major lessons you have learned in life, the guiding principles that are central to your philosophy of life, and the major successes you have experienced.

This story gives Boris a chance to pause and reflect on his life to date. In human years, he has just turned seventy. He has learned a great deal in his time on this earth, and he has accomplished an extraordinary amount, particularly given his rather shaky start to life. While he is proud of what he has accomplished, he realizes he could not have done it alone. He feels humble and lucky.

This story touches on four themes:

➢ Reflecting on the past

➢ Celebrating success

➢ Showing humility

➢ Sustaining effort

In my experience as a person in his seventh decade of life, I feel extremely lucky to have lived as long as I have and to have had the experiences I've had. I was able to raise two wonderful children, enjoy the companionship and support of a loyal and lovely spouse, travel the world, meet exemplary people, read brilliant authors, work on meaningful projects, and have the time to put my thoughts on paper. I am humbled by the challenges of the world and deeply grateful for the opportunities I have had to live, learn, laugh, love, and work.

As a result of responding to this story, you might find yourself engaged with the child in any or all of these questions:

- What are the important lessons you have learned in your life?

- What are you most proud of? How did you celebrate that accomplishment?

- Is there an interest you have on which you have worked hard for a long time?

CHAPTER 39

▼

BORIS CELEBRATES
A MILESTONE

October 22. It was ten years to the day since Boris stumbled into the Hamm yard, a lonely, scared, tired, hungry puppy on a quest. The Hamms, of course, thought that the only quest Boris had was to find food and a safe place to sleep. Little did they know that Boris was not an ordinary dog.

"Let's throw Boris a big party," Liam exclaimed when he realized it was Boris's tenth anniversary in their family.

"Great idea!" Mr. Hamm said. He asked who they would invite.

Aidan shouted out his ideas: "Let's invite Lucky, Prudence, and Gabby."

"Don't forget Zelda," Liam added.

"What about his cat friends?" Mrs. Hamm asked.

"Sally!" Aidan yelled, already very excited about this party.

"What about the squirrels?" Liam teased. They all laughed.

Mr. and Mrs. Hamm spent the entire morning preparing for the party. "Do you think we should have invited any other friends?" Mrs. Hamm asked.

"I think we will have a full house as it is!" joked Mr. Hamm. "I'm a little worried that we don't have enough to eat, though. Those dogs eat like pigs, and Sally and her friends can be pretty catty about their food."

Mrs. Hamm snickered. She noticed that Mr. Hamm was looking rather proud of himself for making his clever jokes. "You're not that funny, you know," she said, winking and enjoying their back-and-forth banter.

When they were all gathered for the party in Hamm's spacious living room, Mrs. Hamm set out bowls of all the guests' favorite foods. She had made lots of sweet corn on the cob. Boris loved corn on the cob. Sally contributed some mushrooms and berries she had found in the woods, but she decided not to bring the mice she had caught that morning.

After everyone had stuffed themselves, Zelda asked Boris, "What are the three most important things you have learned in your ten years here?"

Boris reflected for a while and answered in characteristic fashion: "Restraint, resourcefulness, and respect."

Boris loved to summarize his thoughts in three points with a rhythmic quality. He believed there was a better chance that people might remember if his answers were short and easy to recall. But then, at the urging of the others, he elaborated: "It's important to exercise some restraint on your instincts. Reacting to your first impulse can be dangerous. You need to be resourceful if you want to accomplish your goals. Resources are both internal and external, which means you have to know your strengths and also where you can find support. You have to demonstrate respect for others. It's better to be harder on yourself than you are on others, which means tolerating others' weaknesses and respecting what they do with what they have."

Lucky offered a toast. "Here's to Boris—the dog that convinced the Rogue Rascals to change their name to the Peaceful Puppies!"

"Hear hear!" they all cheered.

"I think we all contributed to that goal," Boris responded graciously, feeling humbled and proud that there had been no violent attacks among any of the gangs since they had all come together, shared their art, and agreed to a peaceful solution. "You never know when another bully may come to town, but at least we learned that it's better to deal with threats as an entire community instead of as individual packs."

"Let's play some games," Liam suggested, trying to be a great host for the party.

"How about Find the Bone?" Aidan said, taking responsibility for making the party go smoothly.

Liam put all the dogs in the garage and hid several bones throughout the yard. As soon as he opened the door, they all scrambled out to see who could find the most.

Sally thought it was unfair because, as a cat, she had no experience hunting for bones.

Overall, it was a great celebration. Boris thought about the day he first arrived. Liam and Aidan were just little boys then. He couldn't believe how they had grown in ten years. His animal friends had all been young. They had all aged, as well.

He remembered how happy he was to have stumbled across Zelda when he made his first daring venture down the path and into the woods. Her advice remained timely and timeless. Boris felt grateful about how much he had learned and how fortunate he was to have chosen the road that led to his neighborhood. Although he felt unsettled because he had never been able to reconnect with his brothers and sisters, he was proud because he'd stayed with his quest to learn as much as he could about life and to help others in the process. It had truly been an excellent ten years.

Guide for Chapter 40:

▼

Boris Becomes a Role Model

In this story, Boris realizes how his behavior impacts others.

In preparation for this conversation, think about the healthiest communities in which you have lived, learned, or worked. What about that community made it easier for you to practice positive health? Was it the culture? Was it a particular role model? Or was it your own motivation and sense of urgency?

This story discusses the changes that Boris's friends have made in their lives because of the example Boris set. There are two key themes in this story:

➢ Creating healthy communities

➢ Understanding how your behaviors impact others

In my experience as a consultant trying to create healthy, innovative, and productive communities, I have found that leadership role modeling and the reward system are the two factors that are most critical to success. People take their cues from their leaders. If leaders are practicing positive health behaviors, people in their organizations are more likely to do the same. As for the second factor, of course people do what they are rewarded for doing. If there are incentives for people to engage in healthy lifestyle behaviors, there is high probability that there will be more enthusiasm for creating a healthy community.

As a result of responding to this story, you might find yourself engaged with the child in any or all of these questions:

- Who is the healthiest person you know? What makes that person so healthy?

- How have you been influenced by the person?

- Do you set an example that others might want to emulate? If you do, what example? If you might not, can you think of a way to begin setting a good example?

- How do expectations in your social groups influence your behaviors?

CHAPTER 40

▼

BORIS BECOMES
A ROLE MODEL

Boris noticed as time passed that Lucky had started reading books, and Gabby had recently been sprinting down the road and jumping into the lake for long swims. Prudence had stopped whining as much as she had in earlier times, and Sally seemed much more confident and secure these days.

Boris was confused, because he couldn't account for these changes in behavior. He hadn't formed any club recently. He had long ago quit trying to convince or harass anyone to improve their exercise or eating habits. He had stopped imposing his beliefs on others. And yet he couldn't help but notice that all the dogs in his neighborhood were trying to get healthier and improve themselves in various ways.

"I'm feeling a lot better since I started exercising," Gabby beamed, her ears flapping in the wind as she dashed down the road, kicking up dust as she went.

"I'm not getting as many stomach aches since I quit eating dead mice and sour berries," Sally volunteered as she crunched on some granola.

"You *so* have to read this book on chasing squirrels," Lucky barked excitedly, hardly able to tear himself away from his new book.

"No complaints from me," Prudence added.

Boris raised his eyebrows and happily offered his support: "You go, Gabby!" he cheered. "Can't wait to read it, Lucky. Glad you're feeling better, Sally. You look stronger, Prudence."

Later, Boris ambled to the pond, shaking his head in amazement at how his neighborhood had turned into a wellness community.

"You didn't think they noticed the way you live your life?" Zelda chided. "It appears that telling doesn't work as well as showing."

Boris gave a grin of satisfaction and said, "Yeah, Zelda, just like you showed me how to stay calm whenever I felt my world was falling apart. Just telling me to calm down would not have helped. What did help was your willingness to be totally present for me and to listen to what I had to say. You stayed so calm that it inspired me to do the same."

After a short talk, Boris strolled back to the Hamm house, enjoying the beautiful scenery as he moved slowly and silently down the path. He admired the blue jay sitting on a branch hanging over the rustic pond. He watched the butterflies play in the wind, floating effortlessly from one spot to another. He noticed the owl sitting peacefully in the tree, calmly watching life go by. Boris felt glad to have become a great role model.

Guide for Chapter 41:

▼

Boris Asks Hard Questions

In this story, Boris learns how to forgive.

In preparation for this conversation, reflect upon the times in your life when you might have felt abandoned, left behind, or ignored.

This story opens up the discussion that has been lurking under the surface of this entire book and Boris's primary, if unexpressed, source of angst: "how could my owner drop me off at the side of the road and expect me to fend for myself?" It addresses four of the major themes that most adopted or abandoned kids have to confront:

➤ Understanding your roots

➤ Creating a balanced perspective

➤ Finding a way to forgive

➤ Moving forward

In my experience as an adoptive parent and knowing many parents with adopted children, I have learned that issues surrounding adoption are always present at some level. Kids want to know the circumstances under which they were born. They want to know details about their biological parents: how old they are, what they are like, their health histories, why they gave their child up for adoption, and what life would have been like if he or she had remained in that family.

Many adopted kids experience real anger, deep hurt, and profound insecurity that gets manifested in a variety of ways. Over time, kids who make a healthy adaptation to their new families reach a balanced perspective: "my biological parents may have been unable to support me even though they loved me, and my adoptive parents must have really wanted me even though I don't have their DNA."

At some point, kids need to find a way to forgive their biological parents for giving them up and their adoptive parents and siblings for not necessarily having the same characteristics and cultural legacy of their biological parents. The fundamental choice for adoptive kids is either to decide to continue to ruminate about what could have been or to mobilize for what could be.

As a result of responding to this story, you might find yourself engaged with the child in any or all of these questions:

- Have you ever felt abandoned or left behind? What did it feel like?

- Have you ever had to forgive someone for hurting you?

- When you have been hurt, how were you able to move forward?

- Have you ever been really angry at what you perceived as the unfairness of life? How did you deal with that anger?

CHAPTER 41

▼

BORIS ASKS HARD QUESTIONS

When Boris returned home from visiting Zelda in the afternoon, he found an unfamiliar car in the Hamms' driveway. Soon he discovered that the car belonged to the woman who had dropped him along the side of the road over ten years ago. Boris felt his stomach flip-flop as the memory flashed in his mind of going out for what he thought would be a nice Sunday afternoon ride, but turned out to be a life-changing experience. The emotional thud of that day still rang loudly in his head and heart.

Mrs. Hamm and the woman, Mrs. Brewer, were talking quietly. Both had serious looks on their faces. Liam and Aidan were outside playing catch. Boris approached the entrance cautiously.

"Did you decide to call him Boris as I had?" Mrs. Brewer asked.

"Boris," Mrs. Hamm answered.

"Oh, my goodness! Is that him?" she asked, spotting Boris ambling up the driveway with a curious look on his face.

"That's our Boris," Mrs. Hamm said fondly.

"He's just as I remembered him, sweet and beautiful." Mrs. Brewer became choked up as she held her heart with one hand and wiped her tears with another. "Come here, Boris," she called. Boris inched slowly up to her, still unsure how he felt or how he should behave.

The woman kneeled down and petted Boris tenderly. "Oh, Boris, you turned out to be a perfect dog. I'm so glad you found such a wonderful home."

Boris noticed the loving kindness in the woman's eyes as he looked up and licked her hand. After embracing the dog tenderly, the woman turned back to Mrs. Hamm and started asking more questions. "How did you find him …?"

Fortunately, Liam and Aidan came over and joined the conversation, easing Boris's discomfort. They proceeded to ask the questions that had been on Boris's mind for so long. "Why did you leave him? How did you think he was going to survive? How many brothers and sisters did he have? What happened to his mother and his siblings?" Some of the questions seemed a bit rude, and Boris noticed that Mrs. Hamm was fidgeting uncomfortably.

"It was the hardest thing I've ever done," Mrs. Brewer began. "We had no money, and I had to make a terrible choice: keep the dogs, or see my kids go hungry. I searched all over for good neighborhoods with lots of children and other dogs. I dropped each of Boris's brothers and sisters in a different neighborhood. I drove through each neighborhood every year to see which family had adopted them and to imagine how each dog was doing.

"When Boris's mother finally passed away, I decided to stop by each house to visit the families and to thank them for providing homes for the dogs. Four of Boris's brothers and sisters are still alive and doing well. One was hit by a car and died a few days later. Another was killed by a gang of nasty dogs.

"As for me, I was eventually able to find a good job, and my kids are healthy. They're getting ready to leave home and go to school."

Boris felt an odd mixture of pain, pleasure, and hope throughout the woman's dialogue. He was sad to hear about his mother and two brothers. It did give him great joy to hear that his first owner had managed to prosper. He felt less rejected when he learned that Mrs. Brewer had loved him but had to give him up, but he was still angry that she had just dropped him on the road instead of finding him a home directly. That still seemed totally irresponsible to him. After hearing some news about them, Boris felt a renewed surge of commitment to connect with his remaining brothers and sisters.

Boris didn't sleep well that night. He kept mulling over in his mind other questions he wished Liam and Aidan had asked. And he started asking himself some hard questions: What am I going to do with the bitterness I have held in my heart for so long? How can I forgive Mrs. Brewer for leaving me, even now that I know she had no real choice? Why didn't she find a home for me instead of just dropping me in the road? How can I open myself up and really trust again?

These were all hard questions to ask … and they were even harder to answer.

GUIDE FOR CHAPTER 42:

▼

BORIS DIGS FOR
HIS BIOLOGICAL ROOTS

In this story, Boris sorts out family relationships.

In preparation for this conversation, reflect upon the relationships you have with your family members.

This story discusses Boris's experience in finding and reconnecting with his biological siblings. Boris discovers that his experiences, and the environment in which he was raised, differ substantially from those of his biological siblings. He is surprised to find out how differently his siblings view the world.

This story deals with three major issues in sibling relationships:

➢ Realizing that the same DNA does not necessarily result in the same beliefs

➢ Deciding the degree of disclosure to use with different relatives. For example, some subjects, like politics and religion, could be better left undiscussed.

➢ Evaluating the impact of environment and experience on behavior and belief.

In my experience as the middle child in a family of three boys, I learned unequivocally that there are profound differences in beliefs in spite of the sameness of our DNA. My older brother grew up in the fifties, became an air force officer and pilot, flew fighter jets in Vietnam, and retired from the military after twenty years. I grew up in the sixties, served three years in military intelligence in Vietnam, joined the Vietnam veterans against the war, and have had multiple careers in the social sciences arena. My younger brother grew up in the seventies, converted to Mormonism after high school, went to medical school in Utah, and set up a family practice office in North Carolina.

All three of us look very much the same, but we could not be more different in our belief systems. We have an agreement not to discuss politics or religion. I'm still trying to figure out how we ended up so different and why each of us feels so strongly about our respective beliefs.

As a result of responding to this story, you might find yourself engaged with the child in any or all of these questions:

- What differences exist among your family members, and how have you dealt with those differences?

- How do you figure out what causes such differences?

CHAPTER 42

▼

BORIS DIGS FOR
HIS BIOLOGICAL ROOTS

Boris was never too interested in digging holes in the ground, but after the visit from his original owner, Mrs. Brewer, he became obsessed with digging for information about his biological brothers and sisters. He had learned from Mrs. Brewer that two brothers and two sisters were still alive and living in not-too-distant neighborhoods. Boris couldn't imagine what they would be like at eleven years old. Strangely enough, though, he was more interested in what they believed than in how they looked.

Searching for his siblings finally gave Boris a chance to put his skateboarding skills to use. Every day he would skate over to a different neighborhood in search of them. After four unsuccessful trips, Boris finally found one of his brothers about three miles from his house. He knew the dog was his brother as soon as he saw him because the dog was a mirror image of Boris. Boris bounded up the hill in anticipation of this long-awaited reunion.

"I'm your brother, Boris!" he called out.

The dog stopped in his tracks, looked at Boris in amazement, dashed over to him, and showered him with licks and snuggles so Boris would know how happy he was to see him. "I'm Bentley," his brother responded enthusiastically. "I'm so glad you found me."

Deliriously delighted with reconnecting, the brothers snuck off to a secluded, shady spot and shared stories of their lives.

Bentley lived in a small town at the top of a long hill that bordered on another beautiful lake. Bentley's family owned luxury cars and fancy boats.

His owners loved dogs and enjoyed travel. They frequently spent the whole summer living on their yacht.

"What's your belief about people?" Boris finally asked, wondering how Bentley viewed the world.

"I think all people are kind and loving," Bentley responded. Boris then shared his beliefs, and the two siblings made plans to meet again sometime soon.

Boris started out on his journey back home. "At least the return trip is downhill instead of uphill!" he thought as he whizzed down the hills, his ears flopping in the breeze. Boris's skateboarding skills sure had improved.

When he returned to the Hamm fam, Boris was empty of energy but full of satisfaction. He had found one of his brothers and learned about his life and his beliefs. After a long period of reflecting on the differences between his life and Bentley's, Boris dug into his plans for finding his other three siblings.

After months of effort and miles of skateboarding, Boris had located Duke, Annie, and Katie. The reunions were all similar: exuberant greetings, long conversations, elaborate planning for the next reunion, and intimate sharing of stories. Boris felt warm inside to get to know his siblings after all these years. He was fascinated by the ways their lives had turned out, and he was stunned by the differences in their beliefs.

"I believe people are mean and nasty," Annie had shared, reflecting on her life living in a materialistic subdivision.

"I believe people are fun and forgiving," Duke concluded based on his experience with an active, sports-minded family.

"I believe people are stupid and selfish," Katie said, thinking about how much time her family spent watching football games and hogging the potato chips.

After Boris left his last reunion, he lumbered home slowly, shaking his head. "We have the same blood, but we sure have different beliefs about some things," he thought to himself.

A few days later, Boris trotted to the pond to share the whole experience with Zelda.

"What do *you* believe?" Zelda asked, feeling fairly confident she knew what her longtime friend would say.

"I think you have to size up each person as an individual. Each person is different, so the way I view one is going to differ from the way I view another. I don't think it's possible to make accurate assumptions or judgments about any group of animals or humans."

"How do you think your siblings came to such different conclusions about how they view the world?" Zelda continued, trying to lead Boris to a greater understanding of his experience.

"That's what I'm confused about," he said as he lay on the ground, chewing on a stick. "Since we all have the same blood, I thought we would probably all have the same beliefs. I guess I was wrong about that."

Zelda responded, "So you were surprised how much your siblings' different environments and experiences had shaped their beliefs?"

"Yes," Boris said, chewing harder on his stick. "We all came from the same parents, but we sure ended up in different places—and not just physically, but mentally, as well."

"And how do you feel about your brothers and sisters now that you know how different your views are from theirs?"

Boris stopped chewing, thought for a few minutes, and finally replied, "I still feel a strong connection and love for them, but I don't feel like I can really open up to them about my beliefs."

"You feel sad, because the relationship is loving, but limited in many ways."

"Exactly," Boris said.

With that he thanked Zelda for her understanding and walked back to the house, deep in thought. "I guess it's possible to love someone with whom you have a deep connection on one level and a shallow connection on another," Boris concluded as he saw the Hamm house at the end of the trail. Regardless, he sure was grateful for the environment and experiences he had with the Hamms.

GUIDE FOR CHAPTER 43:

▼

BORIS CREATES COMMUNITY

In this story, Boris learns how to create a safe and peaceful community.

In preparation for this conversation, reflect upon the different values and norms in the various environments in which you have lived, learned, and worked.

This story discusses how a community can design and implement the kind of culture they want. This could take place via a school-based organization, a neighborhood association, a social service agency, a government institution, a work environment or, in Boris's case, a pack of dogs. Three key themes are covered in the story:

➢ Involving others in the design of the community organization

➢ Creating norms of your own choosing

➢ Defining desired behaviors for the community

In my experience as a culture change consultant, I have found that people are largely unaware of the influence of norms on their behavior and that these norms are far more powerful than they realize. Unfortunately, norms in some environments can suck the soul right out of people. For example, when a company's only value is making money, even if it means engaging in unethical behaviors, that pressure takes its toll on employees' health.

Fortunately, I have also had the experience of helping people create values and norms of their own choosing that have made it much easier for them to act in ways that are life enhancing. In a county jail, we created an environment of respect, discipline, and learning. In a social service agency, we created an environment of trust, excellence, and collaboration. In multiple work settings, we created environments of innovation, teamwork, and quality.

As a result of responding to this story, you might find yourself engaged with the child in any or all of these questions:

- What are the most important values that are present in your social groups?

- How have the groups you're involved with chosen their values?

- How much influence do you think these values and norms have on you?

CHAPTER 43

▼

BORIS CREATES COMMUNITY

Several new puppies had moved into Boris's neighborhood over the past few years. Boris, Lucky, Prudence, and Gabby often heard themselves saying to their frisky new neighbors, "That's not the way we do things around here."

For instance, Boris was disturbed that some of the puppies were mean to the cats. "I saw three of them kick sand on Sally's artwork," he said, shaking his head.

Prudence was upset because sometimes a few of the puppies would gang up on the weaker ones and tease them. "They backed poor Tiffany Terrier into a corner and then nipped at her ears," she said, outraged that they would pick on the smallest new dog in the neighborhood.

Gabby was mad because several puppies had been rude to her. "They left their business outside my doghouse and then ran off laughing," she said peevishly.

Lucky was annoyed at how noisy they were. "They bark all night," he complained, forgetting that he himself was known as The Big Barker. Well, at least Lucky knew when to keep quiet!

"Let's form a Canine Culture Club," Boris finally suggested, reclaiming his own youthful enthusiasm for forming clubs.

"It's been a long time since you've wanted to form a club, Boris, but I think this one may be worth doing. Count me in," Gabby barked.

"Great idea!" Lucky added.

"Okay. Then let's agree to some details," Prudence said, predictability suggesting what she does best.

With Prudence guiding the process, they developed their plan. First, they would invite all the neighborhood's dogs, new and old, to Lucky's house for a community meeting. They would offer juicy bones and diet dog drinks to make sure all the dogs showed up.

"We'd better have some sugar drinks, as well," Gabby suggested, having watched these puppies slurp up the sweet stuff.

"Let's start by asking them what kind of community they would like to create for all the dogs in our neighborhood," Lucky wisely proposed.

After two hours of barking back and forth, they finished their plans. Invitations were sent. They were prepared for the meeting.

The day of the conference arrived, and there was a good turnout. "Welcome to the first meeting of the Canine Culture Club," Boris announced, trying to bring the meeting to order as all the puppies in attendance were eagerly wolfing down as much food as they could stuff into their mouths. With all the barking, biting, scratching, and slurping, it took a long time to get everyone's attention. "What kind of environment would we like to create in this neighborhood?" Boris asked, trying to maintain his calm composure amid all the commotion.

Prudence got the ball rolling. "We should treat all dogs with respect, whether they are young or old."

This statement made the puppies stop what they were doing and pay close attention. "I could go for that," T. J., one of the new puppies, said, seeing that this was not going to be a one-sided event. "In this neighborhood, dogs shouldn't bark at night—unless we see a strange person or dog sneaking around," T. J. added his two cents.

Ears suddenly perked up, slurping stopped, tails wagged, and furry bodies shook. All the younger dogs barked out their ideas enthusiastically. It was fun to create norms they chose for themselves and to have a say in the values they wanted to instill in their community. Instead of living under an abstract idea of "how we do things around here," they defined exactly what they meant by that.

After two hours of intense discussion and debate, the dogs agreed on what was important to them as members of their neighborhood and on ways to know they were behaving in line with the values they'd chosen. They all committed to making these behaviors the standards for their community. Strangely enough, the first letters of each value formed the word *spot*, which reminded them of one of the first books they had heard parents reading to children about dogs. It also helped them remember the four key values.

Safety:

- We look out for the safety of every animal in this community.
- We watch out for strange people and strange dogs.

- We stay out of the street as much as possible.
- We stay alert to cars.

Peace:

- We always try diplomacy first when disputes arise.
- We welcome different colors, sizes, and types of dogs in our neighborhood.
- We appreciate our differences.
- Fighting is a last resort.

Opportunity:

- Every dog has an equal opportunity to learn.
- Every dog has a fair chance for food.
- Each dog has an opportunity to voice his or her opinion.
- We support every dog's quest in life—as long as that quest is not harmful to another.

Trust:

- We do what we say.
- We are honest about what we do.
- We are open with each other.
- We stand up for each other.

Boris asked Sally to create a poster to display all these values and agreed-upon behaviors. Every dog put his or her paw print on the poster, indicating their support. The meeting came to a close—but not before everyone joined in gobbling down a delicious dessert.

GUIDE FOR CHAPTER 44:

▼

BORIS IS CONTENT

In this story, Boris learns to be satisfied with what's present instead of what's missing.

In preparation for this conversation, reflect upon the times in which you have felt envious or longed for an ideal that was unlikely to occur.

This story illustrates how Boris is able to let go of his desires and to be more tuned-in and grateful for what he has. The story covers three major themes:

➤ Accepting what is, not lamenting what isn't

➤ Appreciating the ordinary

➤ Being consistent in your actions despite fluctuating feelings

In my experience as a person always in search of possibilities, I have learned to take delight in whatever the moment brings. I love the Jewish prayer that implores us to say "enough" to whatever life gives us. In my meditations, as I breathe in, I say "I can," and as I breathe out, I complete that sentence with four different statements: "lighten being," "be kind," "extend love," and "smile on." Thus, in four breaths, the goal is to feel lighter, kinder, more loving, and more grateful in each moment.

Even though I try, I still fall short of my goal every day. On many days, I feel heavy, mean, uncaring, and envious. But at least the intention seems right and, with practice, I may get better at controlling those feelings.

As a result of responding to this story, you might find yourself engaged with the child in any or all of these questions:

- Do you ever find yourself sad because something is missing in your life?

- How often do you take time to appreciate all the positive things that are happening in your life? How well do you pay attention to what is positive and meaningful in the ordinary flow of life?

- How satisfied with life do you feel?

CHAPTER 44

▼

BORIS IS CONTENT

Boris had been troubled over the past few days by the greed he observed among the dogs in the neighborhood. Seeing this greed, he reflected upon his earlier years when it seemed like he wanted more of everything, as well. He'd wanted more toys, he'd wanted more bones, he'd wanted more attention, and he'd even wanted a bigger doghouse.

As he turned eleven, Boris noticed that his desires had grown quiet. He was more thankful for each moment: a new smell, a new taste, a new sound, an old friend stopping by, a distant memory, or the old sock he still loved to play with. Just being able to lick his paws gave him great pleasure.

"I wish the Knowleses would build me a bigger doghouse," Lucky complained.

"I wish I had a pretty coat like the new puppy wears when she struts down the road," Prudence whined.

"If only I had more toys to play with," Gabby added. "I'm tired of this squeaking ball the Krafts gave me five years ago."

Boris listened to his friends but made no comment. He found as he grew older that he was content as long as he had water to drink, the sun to keep him warm, beautiful-smelling flowers blooming all around him, and clear air to breathe. "I have enough of everything I need to enjoy life and be grateful."

"Enough," Boris said. He was grateful for the smells of the woods, the breeze off the lake that cooled his furry coat on a hot summer day, and the sounds of water lapping on the pristine, sandy beach that soothed his ears after hearing too much of Lucky's barking. "I have had *enough* of Lucky's barking," Boris chuckled to himself, realizing the double meaning of the word.

"Enough," he said. He had lived for eleven years. He had access to all the information he needed on www.doggie.com, and he had a sharp, clear mind.

"Enough," he said. He enjoyed the music that flowed from his iPod, he loved many of the dogs in the neighborhood, and he still had high hopes for learning more and building deeper connections.

"Enough," he said. His nose could sniff out rabbits, his eyes were as sharp as an eagle's, and he could hear the faintest sounds in the woods when he was out hunting for his favorite mushrooms.

"Enough."

When Boris shared these thoughts with Zelda, she nodded her head and said, "Boris, you've come a long way since we first met all those years ago. You no longer need to be the 'big dog in the neighborhood.' You no longer think you have to be right all the time. And you no longer let your imagination run wild, like being a flying dog or a dancing dog diva."

Boris rolled in the dirt and scratched his ears with his paws, feeling good that Zelda had noticed his changes and was proud of him. "Maybe less is more," he replied with contentment.

"Yes, being totally satisfied with whatever you have makes life easier. Being able to say enough for all your blessings has a much more positive effect than saying enough to all the things that irritate you."

"Oh, Zelda," Boris said. "Life sure is funny."

GUIDE FOR CHAPTER 45:

▼

BORIS SHARES HIS LOVE

In this story, Boris shares his love generously.

In preparation for this conversation, reflect on the people in your life who have shown you genuine affection and those you have shown genuine affection.

This story illustrates the unconditional positive regard that Boris has for others. He gives freely without any expectation of getting something in return. The story has three themes:

➢ Demonstrating loving kindness

➢ Closing emotional distance

➢ Showing positive regard for others

In my experience as a corporate executive, I have found that most work environments are cold and hard places. Generally, there is very little warmth and genuine affection. It's all about business. At the same time, at every place I have worked, I have found warm, caring, supportive people who provide loving kindness. There are usually loving individuals in uncaring environments.

Some people identify with being tough, and there are times when conditions demand making hard decisions. I don't believe that love is unconditional, but I do believe that the world would be a better place if everyone tried to demonstrate loving kindness. It can't be gushy pandering or slurpy affection (like Boris might give); it has to be genuine, authentic, positive regard.

Paradoxically, in this age, people are often looking for trusted advisors. Yet it's impossible to be a trusted advisor without some level of intimacy in the relationship. I believe that demonstrating loving kindness, closing emotional distance, and showing positive regard are three requirements for creating that trust and making the world more productive, peaceful, and prosperous.

As a result of responding to this story, you might find yourself engaged with the child in any or all of these questions:

- Do you have friends who are genuinely warm and affectionate?

- When is it easiest for you to show loving kindness toward another? When is it hardest?

- Do you know anyone who is consistently caring toward others?

CHAPTER 45

▼

BORIS SHARES HIS LOVE

When Boris was a puppy, he always spilled his milk. Now that he was twelve years old, he started spilling his love. While Boris was no longer sloppy with his affection, he still gave it freely—his warmth and caring truly spilled over. And no one scolded him for it.

Boris had experienced love as a puppy. His mother had let him suck at her underbelly. His original owner, Mrs. Brewer, had petted him and held him in her lap. The Hamms had welcomed him into their house. Liam and Aidan would throw balls to him by the hour and play with him. Prudence, Gabby, and Lucky had gone out of their way to make him part of the neighborhood right from the beginning. Finally, Zelda gave Boris attention, support, and wisdom freely and frequently.

Boris returned their love unconditionally. He licked Liam and Aidan's faces every morning. He wagged his tail and wiggled enthusiastically whenever he saw the Hamms. He played endlessly with Lucky, listened for hours to Gabby, discussed art for days on end with Sally, and talked about hundreds of books with Prudence. He never expected anything in return. Boris just figured that was what a dog did.

Boris noticed that humans were not as free with their love as dogs were. Dogs just wanted to lick and snuggle. It seemed that many humans just wanted to debate and fight. Dogs loved to play and entertain. Humans seemed to want to hog all the attention. Dogs warmly showed each other how happy they were to see each other. Humans could be a bit cold and aloof. Dogs loved to touch. Many humans seemed to keep their distance.

Boris decided he liked being a dog. Whenever he noticed coldness in people, (dogs were rarely cold), he showed extra warmth. Whenever he saw distance in someone, he cuddled even closer. Whenever he saw people get stiff, he wiggled all over, wagged his tail, and rolled on the floor. If Boris saw a hand dangling by someone's side, he would run up and lick it. If a person sat down in a chair, Boris would jump right beside him and put his head in the person's lap.

"Boris, you're spilling over with love," Liam said one day, laughing at the dog for going to such extreme measures to make everyone feel loved.

"It's better than spilling my milk," Boris thought to himself.

GUIDE FOR CHAPTER 46:

▼

BORIS REFLECTS ON HIS TRANSFORMATION

In this story, Boris learns the process of changing for the better. He thinks back on his life and realizes how much he has changed. In hindsight, he can see the evolution of his changes for the better.

In preparation for this conversation, reflect on the defining points, or "shocks," that you have experienced in your life that led to transformations of your character.

This story reviews the shocks Boris has had in his life that jolted him into making some life-changing decisions. It covers four themes:

➤ Accepting that shocks happen

➤ Making an effort to improve oneself

➤ Monitoring your thoughts and behaviors

➤ Taking time to relax

In my experience as a change consultant, I have found that a person is more likely to defend their current lifestyle than make the effort to change it. It is also common for people to deny that a change is required or to buffer themselves from the need for change.

The biggest shock of my life came when I was sent to Vietnam. I had enlisted in military intelligence because I had been told that I would be sent to Monterrey, California, for a year of language training and then to

Germany for two years of duty there. Six months later, I stepped out of a transport plane at Tan Son Nhut airport, where I was herded into hot, dusty army barracks in the sticky, humid South Vietnamese environment.

Within the first few months, I realized that what the president of the United States was saying publicly on TV was not an accurate portrayal of what was really going on in the war. I had access to intelligence reports that the general public did not have. Since that time, I have made great efforts to dig for the truth in matters that affect people's lives because I learned that even officials at the highest levels with the most power don't always tell it like it is.

As a result of responding to this story, you might find yourself engaged with the child in any or all of these questions:

- Have you ever been shocked by learning about or experiencing an event? How did that change your life?

- Has a friend of yours ever shocked you with hard, but honest feedback?

- How hard do you work at changing something about yourself based on the feedback you received? How aware are you of your thoughts and feelings about making the changes?

- Do you take the time to think about how your behavior is either helping you achieve your goals or getting in the way of you achieving your goals?

CHAPTER 46

▼

BORIS REFLECTS ON HIS TRANSFORMATION

As Boris grew older, he reflected on his transformation from a lost, exuberant, reckless puppy to a wiser, seasoned leader. He recalled the shocks and effort required along the way.

The first shock came when Boris was dropped off at the top of the hill. The shock of knowing he was on his own and his very survival was up to him was an emotional thud. He went from the warm comfort of snuggling with his brothers and sisters to the cold reality of being lost and alone, a victim of a violent act. Even making the choice of going up the hill or down the hill took great effort. But it made his effort worthwhile whenever he remembered Liam and Aidan yelling out, "Daddy, Mommy! Look at the cute puppy—can we keep him? Please?"

Boris's second shock came when he realized that having talent, working hard, and performing well didn't automatically result in victory. When the judges announced that Boris had not won the dancing dog competition, he couldn't believe it. However, Boris kept working on his dancing skills. Despite a series of disappointing defeats, he eventually learned to simply enjoy creating new steps, even though he never won a trophy. When Prudence had said, "Boris, you did well, and so did Twyla," Boris knew at that moment that life came with no guarantees.

The third shock came when Boris realized that he was more tuned into the faults and weaknesses of others than he was to his own. He learned that love meant more than petting sessions and doggie biscuits; it meant being open, honest, and telling the truth. Zelda was the kindest, wisest, and most trusted dog in the neighborhood, but she could deflate Boris's wild imagination or confront his irrational beliefs quicker than Prudence, Lucky, and Gabby combined.

For instance, it came as a shock to Boris to realize his fanatical belief that dogs could fly couldn't possibly have truth to it. He learned he had to constantly observe his own thoughts and behaviors if he wanted to make progress on his quest for deeper understanding and personal improvement, and he learned he needed to make great effort to seek out the evidence for his beliefs.

When Boris learned that one of his dearest friends saw the world very differently than he did, it provided him with his fourth shock. Even though Boris was crystal clear about what he thought was right, he had learned that Sally Siamese may have had an entirely different view of things. One of the hardest things Boris had to learn in life was to value, accept, and appreciate the differences between individuals.

Boris loved Sally dearly, and she had introduced him to mushrooms, mice, and mysteries that he would have never known without her. When Sally had said, "Boris, you are always judging me and always trying to impose your views on me," Boris was hurt. He had worked hard to deepen that relationship because Sally meant so much to him.

Most importantly, Boris learned that sometimes he preferred being a lazy hound dog instead of a constantly achieving one. He loved to lie in the sun just pawing the wind. He liked taking leisurely walks through the woods and chasing an occasional squirrel here and there. He thoroughly enjoyed lying on the couch licking his fur. Just hanging out with Liam and Aidan gave him great joy. So Boris knew deeply that staying on his quest for improvement not only meant working hard, but also taking time to relax and enjoy. He found that sometimes, *being* instead of *doing* actually accelerated his progress.

Finally, Paul Pitt's sudden death had shocked Boris and taught him about the fragility of life. While the death of a friend is always sad, the shock made Boris even more committed to living life to the fullest.

Boris was proud about how far he had come on his journey. As he reflected on his life with the Hamms and his always-developing ability to stay focused on his goals, he concluded that it was the combination of accepting shocks—or being open to hearing things about himself that he didn't particularly like to hear—and making effort that had gotten him where he was today: lying on the front porch listening to the birds and enjoying the breeze.

GUIDE FOR CHAPTER 47:

▼

BORIS CENTERS HIMSELF

In this story, Boris learns the value of moderation.

In preparation for this conversation, think about a time when you found yourself on an extreme side of an issue or had to deal with someone who was taking an extreme position. Were you able to move to the center or help the other person take a more rational approach?

This story deals with two critical issues: going too fast and taking positions that are too extreme. There are several main ideas taught:

➢ Resisting extremism

➢ Slowing down in order to speed ahead

➢ Thinking more and reacting less

In my experience, I have found that there is a fine line between operating at the margins and taking extreme positions. I believe change occurs at the margins, where innovative ideas advance civilization. This does not mean taking extreme positions. To me, extremism is dangerous because it is often reactionary and irrational. To contrast, operating at the margins means thinking in unconventional ways and pushing the limits of possibility.

Unfortunately, politics and religions universally have extremist groups. One possible problem with religion is that even taking a moderate position legitimizes the extremists. By identifying themselves with Islam, Christianity, or Judaism and providing vast institutional support for these respective creeds, extremists can use their association with and the infrastructure of the religion to support their agendas.

What the world needs are thinkers, not terrorists. Thinkers take their time to process information and generate innovative solutions. On the other hand, rushing in with rash action nearly always has dire results.

As a result of responding to this story, you might find yourself engaged with the child in any or all of these questions:

- When in your experience have you had to deal with an extreme position, like being grounded for a year for not finishing your vegetables? How did you resolve this situation?

- Can you think of a time when you rushed too quickly into a situation and made a mistake because of that?

- How good are you at taking your time to think through challenges, instead of simply reacting to them hastily?

CHAPTER 47

▼

BORIS CENTERS HIMSELF

Boris slowed down as he turned fourteen. He was amazed at how the puppies in the neighborhood seemed to have done just the opposite.

"Hurry up," Henri said as he rushed into the woods, his tail jerking to and fro in anticipation.

And it even seemed to Boris like their games were getting more and more extreme.

"Watch this," T. J. barked as he zoomed straight down the steep hill on his skateboard, fur flying and ears pinned back to his head. T. J. wore goggles, a bright yellow vest, and paw protectors. When he'd hit top speed, T. J. would jump off the board, do a flip, and land with all four paws planted squarely back on the board. Unfortunately, many of his friends ended up at the vet with broken bones after trying these daring feats themselves.

Dancing had even taken on new dimensions for Boris. While the dance moves he had created were innovative at the time, they looked tame in comparison with the gyrations the dogs now performed. Twyla's daughter, Twiggy, now started her dance routine by jumping off a trampoline, flying fifty feet in the air, landing on one paw, and then twirling on her head so fast she became a blur.

"I feel old when I see moves like that," Boris lamented to Prudence, his old dance teacher and friend.

Boris noticed how dog attitudes had changed, as well. Some dogs in the neighborhood were taking extreme positions on one side of an issue or another without getting all the facts. One group of dogs wanted all female dogs to wear clothes that covered all their fur—even on hot days. Some dogs, like relative newcomer Lucy, had even installed video cameras on top of their doghouses so they could monitor all movement.

"I'm afraid someone might sneak up on me when I'm taking a nap," Lucy said, her voice quivering with the fear of some random act of violence. Or even worse, Boris had heard her say, a dog from another neighborhood might sneak in and steal her bone.

Even basic beliefs had changed. One pack believed they would be served endless food in heaven if they died in a gang fight. Another pack believed that all the forces of nature were on its side in its fight for supremacy. A third pack boasted that miracles commonly happened to those who believed in their fancy theories.

Boris found that he had become more centered, calm, and still. Whenever a bunch of dogs came over barking complaints, he would listen carefully and suggest a possible solution. When there was a fighting frenzy over who deserved to get the biggest bone, the world seemed to Boris to turn into a slow-motion film. He could see which dogs were fighting fairly and which ones were biting too hard.

Since Boris was an esteemed elder in the neighborhood, all the dogs came to him to help them solve their problems. In the past, Boris would have jumped into the fray, quickly taking sides and rushing into battle. Now, the more chaos Boris saw in his life, the more centered he became. He was thinking more and reacting less. Oddly enough, as Boris slowed down, problems seemed to get resolved more quickly.

Guide for Chapter 48:

▼

Boris Talks Straight

In this story, Boris protects the environment.

In preparation for this conversation, think about how the environment has changed in your lifetime.

This story addresses a global problem that requires all of us to be more responsible. If poverty, pollution, and industrial production continue to rise, there will be devastating consequences for our global community. Our children are going to inherit these problems and will need to find the solutions. This story suggests three key steps that we can take to deal with this issue:

➤ Owning responsibility for the problems we create

➤ Helping others reach their goals responsibly

➤ Empowering the next generation

In my experience as a father of responsible children, I have seen how young people can mobilize to make a difference. My older daughter started a group in high school called SAVE (Students Against Violating the Environment). This group started a recycling program for the school and heightened student awareness of environmental issues. My younger daughter lived in Ghana for six months under the auspices of UNICEF to study the effects of health, educational, and environmental interventions on people in Africa. In 1992, I wrote a book on ethical leadership that outlined what leaders need to do to combat poverty, pollution, and overproduction. Essentially, the only solution to the problems we are creating right now is to start thinking interdependently and cooperating internationally.

As a result of responding to this story, you might find yourself engaged with the child in any or all of these questions:

- What are you doing to become more responsible about saving the environment?

- How do you think the food we eat gets from the field where it is grown to our tables? How far does each item have to travel? How is it produced?

- Which issue worries you the most: food production, global warming, pollution, species extinction, or population growth?

- Are you doing anything to encourage others to become part of the solution to the problems our society, and our planet as a whole, are starting to face?

CHAPTER 48

▼

BORIS TALKS STRAIGHT

The dog population in the neighborhood had grown. Dogs were worried about getting enough to eat, and messes appeared everywhere.

"Can you believe these puppies don't cover their dog doo with dirt?" Sally said disgustedly after almost stepping in a pile.

Boris was concerned that the neighborhood was not only getting dirtier, it was also starting to smell bad. "I'm worried the grocery stores are going to run out of dog food, so I'm storing as much as I can in my doghouse," several dogs were saying.

"Don't worry," a younger dog, Lucy, said cheerfully. "Everything will work out fine."

Boris decided to call a neighborhood meeting. He met with Prudence, Gabby, Lucky, and Zelda before the meeting to figure the best way to involve and inspire all the dogs in the neighborhood to step up to their responsibilities.

"I'm worried about the environment," Prudence said. "The water in my bowl has been looking cloudy and tasting bad."

"I'm worried that none of the puppies want to read anymore," Gabby lamented.

"When's the last time you saw a puppy run down to the beach and go for a swim?" Lucky added.

"It seems like every dog is just looking out for herself," Zelda said sadly.

Boris knew that giving a speech wouldn't change things, but he felt he had a responsibility to share his point of view. When all the dogs had gathered, Boris thanked everyone for coming.

"There are three things I would like all of us to think about," Boris began. He proceeded to list the issues: "First, we all need to set high standards for responsibility. As members of this community, we need to be clean, caring, and careful. Second, we all need to step up to our own responsibilities. If I make a mess, I should clean it up. Finally, we all need to take responsibility as a community for the problems we are facing."

Lucy and T. J. quit fighting over a sock they had been playing tug-of-war with. "Responsibility?" T. J. asked. "What's that mean?"

"It means you're either part of the problem or part of the solution," Lucy said, looking at T. J. with a scared look in her eyes.

Zelda decided to weigh in. "We have not only been burying our bones, we have also been burying the facts. We all know it's harder to find tasty mushrooms in the woods these days, because there are more of us hunting for fewer mushrooms. And I know that all of us have stepped in some dog poop at some point or other that someone didn't clean up. As more dogs move into this community and bones are harder to find, we need to work together to help each other out. In addition to what Boris suggested, I would add three more things to think about."

Zelda paused before continuing her speech. "First, we can't count on a miracle to solve our problems. The poop we produce is not going to just disappear. Also, sometimes bad things happen to good dogs for no reason. When that happens, we need to pitch in and help. I remember when Gabby had an operation, we all helped her recovery by bringing her toys she could play with that didn't require her to move as much. Last, it's important for us to know that sometimes you are powerless to change what's most important to you. But we need to do what we can, even though there's no guarantee that we will get what we want. We all wish we didn't have to deal with bully dogs, for instance, but sometimes we all have to work together to make sure everyone is as safe as possible."

Boris asked the dogs to break into groups of seven to discuss what they had heard and to come up with their own solutions to the problems facing the community. "Remember," he said, "we older folks will not be around forever to bring you together. You pups will need to assume leadership for this community."

After a time of group discussion, Sally's group explained to the rest what they had decided. "You have to live in the layers of life, not in the litter. I know I have to clean up my litter box," Sally said, "but I would rather spend time in the layers of my art."

The dogs shook their heads, a little confused. But they kept on talking, they kept on thinking, and they kept on coming up with their own ideas for solving their problems. Boris's straight talk had shown the new generation that it was their time to step up and take responsibility.

GUIDE FOR CHAPTER 49:

▼

BORIS THANKS ZELDA

In this story, Boris honors the sources of wisdom in his life.

In preparation for this conversation, think about the people in your life who have really made a difference in the way you view the world.

This story deals with the helplessness we feel in the face of all the horrifying news with which we are often confronted. There are four major themes in the story:

➢ Rising above the "isms" of the world

➢ Conceding to strength—recognizing that other people may have more expertise in a particular area than you do

➢ Knowing what you can change and what you can't

➢ Overcoming the forces of evil

In my experience as a child of the sixties, I learned the importance of questioning authority. I also learned the importance of seeking the truth in my own way. I have come to believe that it is good to trust the seekers of truth and to doubt those who claim to have found the truth. I have been very lucky in my search to have been introduced to many wonderful sources of wisdom and truth. Bob Carkhuff, one of the most cited social scientists of the twentieth century, has been a mentor of mine for almost forty years. I am totally grateful for the wisdom he has imparted to me regarding his search for truth. I have also had the good fortune of being introduced to the amazing writings of Gurdjieff, Ouspensky, Nietzsche, Reich, Rumi, Nicoll, and others. They are all true seekers of truth, and I am humbled in the face their contributions.

As a result of responding to this story, you might find yourself engaged with the child in any or all of these questions:

- What "isms" do you find most difficult to deal with in day-to-day life? For example, racism, materialism, or sexism?

- Who has a strength you really admire? Do you try to compete with them or learn from them?

- Have you ever decided you were not capable of changing a situation? How did it feel?

- How could you mobilize your friends to overcome an evil in the world?

CHAPTER 49

▼

BORIS THANKS ZELDA

Boris woke from his nap (his naps had grown longer and become more frequent) and stretched his old body. Even though Boris still exercised regularly, his muscles took longer to loosen up nowadays, and he didn't have the instant zip that he had as a puppy. He knew that his days on this earth were getting shorter.

Boris wanted one last philosophical conversation with Zelda. Although Boris still had a steady mind, his feet were a bit unsteady as he made his way to the pond where Zelda still lived. "Zelda, my friend, it's good to see you."

"It's good to see you, Boris. We've been friends for a long time. I'm glad you made the effort to come visit. I always enjoy our conversations."

"Zelda, I just wanted to thank you for being so kind to me all these years and for providing me with such wise guidance. Life would have been so much different—and so much less—without you."

"Well, Boris, the respect is mutual. I have always loved your inquiring mind and your gentle soul. I have learned from you, as well. We may have less pep these days, but together, we have developed a deeper perspective."

"I was thinking the other day how much more difficult it is to raise a child than to raise a dog," Boris said. "If people provide a warm, loving, supportive environment for us dogs, we will respond in kind. Our love seems to be more unconditional and constant. I think it's much more difficult for parents like the Hamms. They provide a loving environment for Liam and Aidan, but there are so many other influences in their lives that it's impossible to predict how they will turn out."

"That's a good insight," Zelda responded. "There is so much violence, racism, sexism, materialism, and militarism to contend with in the world. All these 'isms' make raising a child more difficult than raising a dog. You never know which 'ism' might poison the child. But as for us dogs, most of us just care about getting fed and getting petted every now and then."

"You're right, Zelda. I have always appreciated your ability to understand what I have said and to raise the conversation to another level." Boris felt good letting Zelda know how much he valued her. He continued, "It's difficult to know what you can change and what you can't change. For dogs, that's easy. For people, it's not. I know the Hamms are terribly distressed by all the conflicts around the world. They do what they can by sending money to relief agencies, but it doesn't seem to make much of a difference. They must feel so helpless.

"It's sad when the forces of good are not sufficient to overcome the forces of evil. I hope the young people of this generation will be able to use all the new technology and tools they have developed to create a more harmonious world. Things are simpler for dogs. We just have to know when to wag our tails and when to bark." The two companions both laughed at that comment.

"Boris, I have always loved your eagerness to learn and your willingness to concede to dogs who had more knowledge or skills in an area you wanted to learn about—like dancing, flying, or teaching," Zelda said.

Boris and Zelda looked deeply into each other's eyes, knowing that this could be one of their last conversations. Boris wagged his tail, touched noses with Zelda, and returned to his doghouse at the Hamms' with an occasional bounce in his step and a constant peace in his heart.

GUIDE FOR CHAPTER 50:

▼

BORIS FACES HIS OWN DEATH

In this story, Boris finds peace.

In preparation for this conversation, reflect upon your experience with death. Who was the first person or pet you lost? How did the bluntness of that reality shape your view toward life? What legacy do you want to leave behind when you die? Do you think you are able or will be able to see death as just another moment?

This story deals with the ultimate reality we all face. Life is finite. We have a limited time. We all have to deal with the fact that our lives will end. The story covers three goals we need to consider as we face our own mortality:

➢ Growing old gracefully

➢ Seeing death as just another moment

➢ Building a legacy to leave behind

In my experience as an adult in his sixties who has lost both parents and in-laws, I feel lucky that all four of them lived fully into their eighties and died without extended hospitalization or pain. My dad was still waterskiing in his seventies, and my mother-in-law played tennis and went to yoga in her eighties. None of them was a burden, and none was bitter about life. I feel so grateful for the positive influence they had on my life.

My mother-in-law was almost ninety-two when she passed. She experienced heart failure and was taken to the hospital. Three days later, she went to a wonderful hospice care setting. In her last lucid moments, as her grandchildren held both of her hands, she smiled, her face brightened, and she said, "This is everything, this is everything." To her, death was just another beautiful moment.

As I enter the last phase of my life, I hope I will be able to grow old and die with as much dignity and grace as my parents and in-laws. In the meantime, I'm trying to build a legacy with my books, my relationship to my family, and by the impact I have on the individuals and organizations with whom I work.

As a result of responding to this story, you might find yourself engaged with the child in any or all of these questions:

- Who do you know who has aged gracefully?

- What do you hope to contribute to this world during your lifetime?

- What would it take for you to be able to see death as just another moment, rather than as the *last* moment?

CHAPTER 50

▼

BORIS FACES HIS OWN DEATH

Boris was feeling mellow after his fifteenth anniversary with the Hamm fam. They had thrown him another party, and he felt warm inside knowing how much they had cared for him over the years.

"I guess we won't have any wild games at this party," Aidan had said, making the obvious observation that the neighborhood puppies no longer lounged around in the living room.

Life had changed since Boris first arrived. Liam was off to college. Aidan was starting twelfth grade. The Hamms parents now had gray hair and moved more slowly. And Boris was feeling his age, as well. His legs were shaky when he first stood up. He didn't have the bounce in his step like he did as a puppy. He no longer chased squirrels with Lucky, whom he now referred to affectionately as Limpy. Boris felt all the general aches and pains of growing old.

Even with more aches and less energy, Boris continued to grow as a student of life. He still read as many books as he could with his new eyeglasses, and his book group still met every month, even though Gabby talked less and Prudence couldn't remember as much as she once did. "What was the point of that book?" Lucky would grumble when he didn't quite understand the message.

In spite of the maladies and memory loss, Boris's relationship with the dogs in his neighborhood had deepened over the years. He also still walked to the pond every day to visit Zelda, although there was more lumbering than leaping these days.

Boris particularly treasured his walks in the woods because he took the time to appreciate the flowers, birds, and changes that were taking place in the forest. While he was in no rush to get to the pond, he still valued his relationship with Zelda, who remained as wise as ever through the years. They talked about how life had changed as they had grown old together, how they were thankful for each moment they'd had, and how life here would soon come to an end. "Death is just another moment," Zelda would say as they came to grips with the ultimate reality for everyone on earth.

"Mom, where's Boris?" Aidan asked one day when Boris didn't show up for breakfast.

"That's strange," Mrs. Hamm replied with a concerned tone, knowing that Boris never missed a meal.

When they went to check on Boris in his bed, they noticed that he wasn't moving. Aidan quickly went over and put his hand on Boris's heart. "It's not beating," Aidan cried. He knew then that Boris had died peacefully in his sleep. He and Mrs. Hamm gave each other a big hug and wept tears of sadness.

"He was a great dog, and he had a great life," Mrs. Hamm finally said, trying to comfort Aidan.

"I really loved that dog," Aidan said. They shared the news with Mr. Hamm and Liam and made the final arrangements.

It was one of largest dog funerals ever held. All of Boris's old friends managed to attend, of course, and all the new puppies came, as well. They had all grown to admire and love Boris, who was clearly seen by all as the elder leader. Packs of dogs from other neighborhoods all came to pay their respects. They appreciated the work Boris had done to establish peace in their world. Even the remains of the Rogue Rascals came. They had become part of the community and were now working with the other neighborhood packs to deal with a new gang that was threatening their safety.

They all shed tears of grief and barks of gratitude when Zelda shared her thoughts at the service. "Here lies a dog whose quest was to seek the extraordinary. He showed us all how to lead, how to love, and how to laugh. Throughout his whole life, he hoped for a better world. He helped others attain that dream, and he helped heal the community's wounds in the process. Boris truly knew how to live, and he knew how to die. May his soul rest in peace."

Epilogue

▼

Boris Gets a Namesake

Aidan drove to the basket and let the ball roll off his fingertips. The ball bounced gently off the backboard and went cleanly through the hoop—swish! "Yes!" Aidan yelled as he clenched his fist and punched the air in sweet satisfaction.

"Try to get a little more height on your jumps," Liam instructed from the bleachers, proudly watching his younger brother dominate the game as he held hands with Sarah, his fiancée.

It was hard to believe that five years had gone by since Boris died. It was Aidan's senior year in college. Liam and Sarah had graduated from college and had come home to watch Aidan's last game playing for the local university's team. Mr. and Mrs. Hamm beamed as their boy raced down the floor to defend his bucket, determined to win the conference championship.

Meanwhile, Junior was panting and puffing at the Hamm house in anxious anticipation of the family's return. It turned out that T. J. and Lucy had had a love affair. Junior was one of the happy results of their brief union. The Kraft and Roh families presented the Hamms with Junior just as soon as Lucy had weaned him. The Hamm fam was delighted with this young, frisky puppy.

"Junior is just as enthusiastic and wiggly as Boris was at that age," Aidan reflected.

"Yeah, I remember when Boris just couldn't contain himself. He was always running around the house with wild delight and making our parents crazy," Liam added.

"Boris was always a lot of fun as a puppy, and he turned into the best dog ever. You never knew what kind of scheme Boris would come up with next."

Aidan and Liam smiled as they shared these wonderful memories of Boris.

The Fables of Boris Live On

Another five years passed.

Liam and Sarah had splurged on a big family vacation to Hawaii to celebrate their fifth anniversary.

"That's the biggest booger I ever saw," Felix said to Anna Bell.

Sarah wiped Anna Bell's nose, and Liam told Felix to quit picking on his little sister.

The pristine Hawaiian beach crunched under the young kids' tiny feet as the warm saltwater washed their little toes.

"Hey, Uncle Aidan, will you come build sand castles with us?"

"Sure," Aidan said. "I can't think of anything I'd rather do."

"Daddy, please tell us again how Boris was dropped off at the top of the hill and managed to find your house," Felix pleaded.

Liam and Aidan retold the story for the twentieth time. Felix and Anna Bell sat motionless on the beach with their eyes wide open as they listened to every detail about Boris starting out on his quest.

Anna Bell pulled her thumb out of her mouth just long enough to beg, "Daddy, Daddy, just one more Boris story."

APPENDIX

▼

AN OVERVIEW OF LEARNING
OBJECTIVES AND LIFE SKILLS

Chapter	Title	Page	Objective	Life Skills
1	Boris's New Life Starts with a Thud	3	To begin the quest for spiritual development and growth	➤ Making decisions ➤ Staying calm in a crisis ➤ Looking for possibilities in even the worst situations ➤ Taking the initiative to make things happen in your life
2	Boris Settles in to His New Neighborhood	9	To learn and understand the rules	➤ Welcoming new people into a community ➤ Dealing with new places, new people, and new rules ➤ Knowing what "the rules" are
3	Boris Finds a Wise friend	15	To find people from whom you can learn	➤ Keeping your mind open ➤ Identifying friends you can trust
4	Boris Breaks the Rules	21	To dive into the layers and complexities	➤ Deciding when to let yourself free and when to control your actions

5	Boris Assesses His Current Life	25	To stay open to the whole truth	➤ Observing how friends can sometimes stew in their reality or ignore their possibilities ➤ Seeking possibilities responsibly ➤ Being harder on yourself than others ➤ Seeking counsel on difficult issues
6	Boris Makes a Plan	31	To pursue your dreams	➤ Setting goals ➤ Finding the right teacher ➤ Assessing your talents ➤ Dealing with setbacks ➤ Giving honest feedback
7	Boris Contemplates Freedom	37	To define what it means to be free	➤ Being who you are ➤ Thinking what you want to think ➤ Saying what you want to say ➤ Exploring feelings you may have ➤ Acting how you want to act
8	Boris Connects to a Higher Purpose	43	To search for meaning in life	➤ Defining a mission outside oneself ➤ Brainstorming possibilities ➤ Finding meaningful work ➤ Promoting an idea ➤ Sustaining change
9	Boris Recalls His Early Puppyhood	47	To bring back joyful memories	➤ Recalling memories ➤ Defining the simple principles of life ➤ Giving love freely ➤ Using all the senses to find joy ➤ Resolving unanswered questions

10	Boris Clears his Mind and Thinks Positively	51	To learn the power of meditation	➤ Being grateful for every day we are given ➤ Confronting negative behavior ➤ Thinking positively ➤ Meditating peacefully ➤ Living in the world, but not being of the world
11	Boris Helps Create Peace	57	To find peaceful solutions	➤ Resisting cultural norms (dealing with peer pressure) ➤ Innovating and staying open to nontraditional or unconventional ideas ➤ Finding healthy exceptions to the rules
12	Boris Discovers the Problem with Relationships	63	To figure out the root causes of problems	➤ Being open to new adventures ➤ Looking beyond idiosyncrasies ➤ Sharing decision making ➤ Agreeing on truth and blame
13	Boris Manages His Impulses	69	To decide which instincts to free and which to restrain	➤ Closing down primal instincts ➤ Dealing with hormonal changes ➤ Observing your thoughts and feelings ➤ Choosing how to act on those thoughts and feelings ➤ Listening to your conscience
14	Boris Expects Better from Himself	73	To improve your level of functioning in all dimensions of life	➤ Seeking wholeness ➤ Making a strong effort ➤ Wishing versus working ➤ Assessing your abilities
15	Boris Advocates for Gratitude	79	To be grateful for your gifts	➤ Being grateful ➤ Creating your own story ➤ Dealing with negativity ➤ Confronting victimhood

16	Boris Learns How to Learn	85	To take charge of your own learning	➤ Making deeper connections ➤ Getting to the root causes ➤ Overcoming one's history and bad habits ➤ Learning how to learn ➤ Inquiring without irritating
17	Boris Considers Himself in the Mirror	89	To develop a crystallized sense of self	➤ Unifying your being
18	Boris Meditates	95	To learn how to relax	➤ Creating your own space ➤ Finding time for yourself ➤ Practicing relaxation
19	Boris Sizes Up His Friends	99	To leverage your strengths and manage your weaknesses	➤ Dealing with differences ➤ Owning your strengths ➤ Confronting your deficits
20	Boris Believes He Can Fly	103	To test beliefs against the evidence	➤ Seeking out evidence for your beliefs ➤ Respecting others' rights to believe what they want ➤ Opening yourself up to possibilities
21	Boris Learns about Leadership	109	To make a difference through effective leadership	➤ Assessing level of functioning ➤ Finding support for your ideas ➤ Identifying the right talent for a job ➤ Creating an environment that supports your goals
22	Boris Makes a Soul	115	To create a soul	➤ Being careful about what you wish for ➤ Resisting the need for attention and self-indulgence ➤ Staying true to who you are

23	Boris Tries to Inspire Others	121	To give much to a world that wants so little	➤ Modeling your behaviors on the right behaviors and attitudes ➤ Remembering who you are talking to ➤ Entering the frame of reference of others before you try to educate them
24	Boris Teams Up with His Friends	125	To value collaboration	➤ Engaging others ➤ Sharing ideas ➤ Being open to others' ideas ➤ Building on others' ideas ➤ Empowering others to lead
25	Boris Catches Himself Stretching the Truth	131	To tell the truth	➤ Describing your experiences objectively ➤ Resisting hyperbole
26	Boris Wakes Up	135	To increase consciousness	➤ Being fully present in the moment ➤ Paying close attention to surroundings and events ➤ Connecting deeply to other people
27	Boris Moves Up the Scale	139	To change your goals as you become older and wiser	➤ Setting realistic goals ➤ Growing as others grow, or even if they don't
28	Boris Gets It Together	143	To clarify values and set priorities	➤ Clarifying your values ➤ Prioritizing your time usage to meet your goals ➤ Engaging life in multiple dimensions
29	Boris Takes a Risk	147	To learn the difference between risk taking and thrill seeking	➤ Practicing for perfection ➤ Pushing yourself or someone else when they need a push ➤ Assessing risks and learning not to arbitrarily seek thrills

30	Boris Shows Compassion	153	To suspend judgment	➤ Observing your judgments to make sure they are fair ➤ Growing a big heart, mind, and soul ➤ Keeping an open mind ➤ Being harder on yourself than you are on others
31	Boris Takes the Initiative	159	To learn that success requires both opportunity and initiative	➤ Creating the conditions that enable your quest for personal improvement ➤ Seizing opportunities when they arise
32	Boris Suffers a Loss	165	To deal with death	➤ Keeping memories alive ➤ Telling the whole truth about a person's life ➤ Dealing with the reality of our mortality ➤ Living with death on your shoulder ➤ Transforming darkness into light
33	Boris Discovers the Importance of Doubt	169	To learn that gray is more likely than black or white	➤ Embracing uncertainty ➤ Conducting good research ➤ Seeking out multiple sources ➤ Creating a balanced perspective ➤ Resisting generalizations
34	Boris Lightens Up	175	To let go of negative emotions	➤ Observing your mood ➤ Letting go of negative emotions
35	Boris Adjusts His Expectations	179	To laugh at yourself	➤ Setting realistic goals ➤ Being able to laugh at yourself
36	Boris Learns to Appreciate Differences	183	To value differences between people and modify your style	➤ Viewing individual differences as gifts ➤ Flexing your personal style
37	Boris Finds the Courage to Act	189	To find the courage to act	➤ Stepping up in a crisis

38	Boris Practices Diplomacy	193	To seek peaceful solutions to all problems	➤ Building a coalition of strength ➤ Leveraging individual strengths for the greater good ➤ Seeking peaceful solutions ➤ Maintaining a vigil for evil
39	Boris Celebrates a Milestone	199	To give thanks for what you have	➤ Reflecting on the past ➤ Celebrating success ➤ Showing humility ➤ Sustaining effort
40	Boris Becomes a Role Model	205	To realize how your behavior impacts others	➤ Creating healthy communities ➤ Understanding how your behaviors impact others
41	Boris Asks Hard Questions	209	To learn how to forgive	➤ Understanding your roots ➤ Creating a balanced perspective ➤ Finding a way to forgive ➤ Moving forward
42	Boris Digs for His Biological Roots	213	To sort out family relationships	➤ Realizing that the same DNA does not necessarily result in the same beliefs ➤ Deciding the degree of disclosure to use with different relatives ➤ Evaluating the impact of environment and experience on behavior and belief
43	Boris Creates Community	219	To create a safe and peaceful living environment	➤ Involving others in the design of a community organization ➤ Creating norms of your own choosing ➤ Defining desired behaviors for the community
44	Boris Is Content	225	To be satisfied with what you have	➤ Accepting what is, not lamenting what isn't ➤ Appreciating the ordinary ➤ Being consistent in your actions despite fluctuating feelings

45	Boris Shares His Love	229	To give love generously	➤ Demonstrating loving kindness ➤ Closing emotional distance ➤ Showing positive regard for others
46	Boris Reflects on His Transformation	233	To learn the process for personal improvement	➤ Accepting that shocks happen ➤ Making an effort to improve oneself ➤ Monitoring your thoughts and behaviors ➤ Taking time to relax
47	Boris Centers Himself	237	To slow down	➤ Resisting extremism ➤ Slowing down in order to speed ahead ➤ Thinking more and reacting less
48	Boris Talks Straight	241	To protect the environment	➤ Owning responsibility for the problems we create ➤ Helping others reach their goals responsibly ➤ Empowering the next generation
49	Boris Thanks Zelda	245	To honor the sources of wisdom in your life	➤ Rising above the "isms" of the world ➤ Conceding to others' strengths or expertise ➤ Knowing what you can change and what you can't ➤ Overcoming the forces of evil
50	Boris Faces His Own Death	249	To find peace	➤ Growing old gracefully ➤ Seeing death as just another moment ➤ Building a legacy to leave behind
Epilogue	Boris Gets a Namesake	251		
Epilogue	The Fables of Boris Live On	253		

Breinigsville, PA USA
26 October 2009
226439BV00001B/5/P